BRAWLER

Scott Hildreth

Published by
Eralde Publishing

Cover Design Copyright © Creative Book Concepts
Text Copyright © Scott Hildreth
Formatting by Creative Book Concepts

ISBN 13: 978-0692722688

DEDICATION

Family. Not an easy thing to embrace at all times. But, in the end, there's no replacement.

Whether you're bound by blood or by bond, this one is for you.

PROLOGUE

Cheerios. Ten or so of them floating in a bowl of milk. That's my earliest memory. I don't know how old I was at the time, but I was younger than two years old. I'm sure of it, because the next vivid recollection I have is of my second birthday. I don't recall the gifts I received, but I'm sure I was two. Either that, or my father could only afford two candles. There was frosting. Lots of frosting. And wrapping paper.

Following my second birthday was loud music. Kisses. Fizzy drinks. The blue car with multi-color cloth interior. The smell of sweat. A mustache. Band-Aids. The house with no trees. Rain that lasted forever. A boxing ring. The house with nothing but trees. A bicycle. Macaroni and cheese. And bunkbeds. I never understood the bunkbeds, but then again, I never asked.

And then, nothing until I was seven. Second grade with Emily Barton. We got in a fight in the hallway over something so unimportant I couldn't recall it a week later, and damned sure can't remember now. I'll never forget how much it hurt to have my hair pulled, though.

Elementary and middle school must have been uneventful, because I really don't remember much between Emily pulling my hair and the first day of high school.

High school brought with it football, house parties, and boys. Bobby Breyton talked me into giving him head in the back of Toby Wilson's truck when I was a freshman. He later told everyone what a slut I was. At first, I denied it. In time I learned admitting to it made me much more marketable, so I proudly laid claim to the house party truck bed blowjob. An overabundance of sexual opportunities soon followed. Hoping to find love, I took advantage of most of them.

Love, however, remained elusive.

My sophomore year, my life was disrupted. From that point through my senior year, life was a blur of boys, beer, blowjobs, and being backhanded by my father.

I left home the day after I graduated high school.

I was eighteen. Eighteen and angry.

It was 1,057 miles from my home in Omaha, Nebraska to Corpus Christi, Texas, and Corpus Christi was my final destination. I wanted to see the beach. I made it as far as Austin, Texas. It was a far cry from the Gulf of Mexico, but at the time I saw it as the beginning to what I was certain would end up being a perfect life.

I was getting coffee. He was leaving when I was going in. We collided. At that moment, I was 18 and he was 31. I was certain we were placed on the earth for one another. We both liked coffee.

And wild sex.

Preston was handsome, rich, treated me well, and fucked me hard. At least at first. Time passed quickly. Every day it seemed things got better. Not that they were ever bad. In fact, they were great.

From there things got better than great.

Spectacular.

Yes. My life changed from a fairly miserable existence to being spectacular.

And then things went to shit. Not over a period of time, or after a sequence of events, but immediately. One day he simply decided he'd had enough. And just like that...

My life with him was over.

He kicked me to the curb. Not a metaphorical curb kicking. He actually kicked me to the curb. Love, I learned, was something glorified in story books and fairy tales.

In real life, it simply didn't exist.

With a backpack filled with my personal items and a little money he gave me to *get on my feet*, I went from the comfort of his million-dollar home to living alone in a one-bedroom apartment.

I didn't live there for long. In a short period of time, I had the world by the balls.

How?

I beat the shit out of a guy for trying to steal my backpack at Starbucks. Before he had a chance to wipe the blood from his lips, I met a man who volunteered to train me as a professional fighter. And, through him, I met another man. The man who proved to me that love was real.

The trainer who noticed my raw talent?

His name's Mike.

It's short for Michael.

But no one ever calls him by his name.

They call him Ripp.

My name's Beth, but no one ever calls me by my name, either.

They call me Jaz.

It's short for Jasmine.

This is my story. It's about fighting, fucking, and falling in love.

In that order.

ONE

JAZ

Day one.

Spring in Austin was a perfect time to sit at the coffee shop and people watch. It was one of the few social events I enjoyed doing, but the tattooed asshole holding my backpack had me wondering if I had chosen the wrong place to do it. I'd made the mistake of leaving it in the outside seating area while I went inside to pee. When I came out, it appeared he was preparing to leave with my stuff.

Dressed in a sleeveless black tee shirt, jeans, and biker boots, he was covered from his neck to his fingertips with tattoos. The stocking cap pulled down low on his head was well out of season, and told me he was either a dip-shit or a thug.

I snatched my backpack from his grasp. "You shouldn't mess with other people's shit."

"I thought someone left it."

Bullshit, you were going to steal it.

"Someone did leave it," I said, my tone angry and bitter. "Me. I walked inside and went to the bathroom. It doesn't make it public fucking property."

I tossed it onto the table beside me and shot him a glare.

He shrugged. "You shouldn't leave your shit laying around."

I had zero interest in listening to his reasoning. "If something's not yours, don't fuck with it."

A fire engine red old-school muscle car pulled into the lot. With exhaust so loud it shook the ground and music blaring from the open windows, it caused both of us to shift our attention toward the sound.

The car came to a stop. An over-sized gym rat with a shaved head and tattoos got out of the driver's door. Another man – who looked like he belonged on the cover of a men's fitness magazine – got out the other side.

I reluctantly tore my eyes from the handsome passenger and focused on the idiot I was arguing with. "Are we done?"

"If you're done being a bitch."

I cocked my hip. "Excuse me?"

"You heard me."

"I wasn't being a bitch. It's my stuff, and you were fucking with it."

Still deep in my personal space, and only a few feet from the table where my pack was lying, he chuckled a shitty little laugh. "You're a mouthy little bitch."

Regardless of what his tattoo artist might have told him, having the tattoos didn't make him any tougher. When a douchebag gets tattoos, he becomes a tattooed douchebag, and as far as I was concerned, that's all he was.

I dropped my gaze to his feet and slowly took every inch of his lanky frame into view. As my eyes met his, I let him know how much I respected his opinion. "Fuck you," I hissed.

His eyes shot to the bag and his hand quickly followed. My instinct was right. He was nothing more than a common thief, and he was trying to take my shit. As he turned to run with the pack, I balled my fists, clenched my jaw, and did what seemed natural.

I fought for what was mine.

I swung a fading left jab just to see how he reacted, and followed it up with a right uppercut. The second punch connected perfectly with his chin, and stopped him from taking even one more step. His eyes went glassy, his hands dropped, and my backpack fell to the ground.

As easy as it would have been to leave it at that, I didn't. While he stumbled and tried to regain his footing, I planted my feet and looked for an opening. He didn't make me wait long. His right hand raised instinctively to try and protect himself.

As soon as his elbow cleared his ribcage, I swung another hard punch.

What do you think of this, motherfucker?

The breath shot from his lungs in one loud burst. Now teetering with his head at the height of my chest and his eyes glassy and unfocused, I knew one more punch would end it for him. I had every intention of doing just that – ending it. I swung a ferocious right hook. The punch connected perfectly with his left eye, knocking him into a stumbling series of steps.

Rocked hard by the barrage of quick punches, his brain was no longer able to control his muscular functions. He and his tattoos fell in a pile on the sidewalk.

I shook my aching hands and glared down at the wad of human waste. "Got your ass kicked by a fucking girl, didn't you?"

"What the fuck happened?" someone from behind me asked.

The voice was thick with a Texas accent, something I didn't have – or want. I picked up my backpack and spun around. Baldy stood a few feet away, shaking his head. He was massive, but now that he was close enough to touch, he seemed like a big teddy bear.

I raised my pack. "He was trying to take my stuff."

He rested his hands on his hips and stared down at the tattooed idiot. "Tryin' is about right. Jesus, you kicked that poor dude's ass six ways from fuckin' Sunday."

Wearing cargo shorts and a wife beater, he looked like a typical meathead – shaved head, goatee, tattoos, and muscles on top of muscles. The only thing about him I liked was that he was wearing a pair of Ed Hardy Chuck's. I admired them for a moment, glanced down at my worn out shoes and wished I could afford a new pair.

"Your hands are quick as a motherfucker, girl," he said, the tone of his voice matching the excitement in his eyes. "Where the fuck'd you learn to fight like that?" he asked.

"In a boxing ring."

The human tattoo managed to stand up. He spoke his mind, but only after he stepped well beyond my reach. "Fucking bitch."

Baldy folded his arms in front of his massive chest and stepped between us. "Kick rocks, motherfucker. Or I'll start beatin' on ya."

Dip-shit picked up his stocking cap, pulled it down low on his head, and mumbled to himself as he turned away.

I tossed my backpack over my shoulders and glanced toward where I expected my coffee to be. Overturned on the sidewalk, the cup was empty.

Fuck.

It may not have seemed like much, but to someone on an extremely fixed budget, the cup of coffee was pretty big deal. A luxury.

"What's your name?" Baldy asked.

"Jaz."

"I'm Ripp," he said excitedly. "Don't go anywhere."

I stood filled with wonder while he ran to his car. He quickly returned with a business card. "I train boxers. You ever fight pro?"

I chuckled. "Nope. Just when people piss me off."

"Wanna consider it?"

I glanced at the card. Fighting pro seemed like something the professionals should be doing, not me. I acted interested nonetheless. "Does it pay?"

"Depends on how good you are."

I clenched my fists and raised them. "How good am I?"

He grinned a cheesy grin. "Good enough you've got my interest, that's for fuckin' sure."

His free use of the f-word and the excitement in his voice made me feel comfortable. At least he wasn't trying to sugar coat who he was. I bent down and picked up my empty coffee cup. "Buy me a cup of coffee, and I'll listen to what you have to say."

He tossed his head toward the entrance. "Come on."

Dressed in sweat pants and a *Kidd's Gym* tee shirt, his handsome friend stood quietly by the door. I snuck a quick look. He had an early summer tan, dark hair and the muscular structure of a boxer. He was so perfectly good-looking that his mere existence was sure to intimidate women, me included.

Ripp slapped him on the shoulder. "Ethan, this is Jaz."

I glanced at Ethan. It was the biggest mistake I'd made in a year. He met my gaze. His blue eyes sucked me in like a vacuum. I stood there, frozen. Lust leeched from my pores.

I tried to look away, but didn't totally succeed. "Nice to meet you," I murmured.

He grinned and pulled the door open. "Nice hands."

You've got nice eyes.

And a terrific ass.

I walked past him, but my eyes stayed locked on his. I broke his gaze immediately before I walked into the edge of the cashier's counter. I felt like a love drunk teen. I probably looked like one, too. I realized I had yet to acknowledge his comment about my quick hands, so I did.

Feeling slightly self-conscious about my chipped fingernail polish, and wishing I had taken time to fix them before I went out, I shoved my hands into the pockets of my shorts. "Thanks."

If being trained by Ripp included anything to do with Ethan, I was all for it. We got our drinks, went back outside, and sat in the sun. I tried to focus on what Ripp was saying and not gawk at Ethan. Not looking at him entirely was impossible, so I took an awkward glance each chance I got.

"So what do you think?" Ripp asked.

Ethan was gazing into the street, obviously in deep thought. I was making note of how his shirt clung to his chest, in deeper thought. I tore my eyes away and met Ripp's gaze. "About?"

He took a drink of his coffee and winced in disgust. "Were you listenin' to what I was sayin?"

"I think I faded off for a second," I said. "Lack of sleep."

"I said we ain't got enough girls in the sport, and if you come to the gym and let me see you spar with one, I'll let you know what I think."

"And then what?"

Ethan shifted his focus to the conversation. I did my best to act like I didn't care. For some reason, though, I did.

"If you're as good as I think you might be I'll train ya."

"I don't have any money," I said.

10

It sounded like I was destitute. I was pretty close, but I didn't want them to know it. Before he responded, I corrected myself. "I meant I don't have any money that I want to spend on lessons or whatever."

He tossed his cup of coffee high into the air and pointed toward the trash can twenty feet away.

"Five bucks," Ethan shouted as soon as the cup left his grasp.

Ripp grinned. "Bet."

The cup fell directly into the trash can. A one in a million shot.

Ripp slapped his hand down on the table. "Pay up."

While Ethan dug for his wallet, Ripp grinned his cheesy grin. "Won't cost you a cent. If you're as good as I'm hopin', I'll train ya for free. I'll get some fights set up, and who knows? Maybe you'll fight for the title one day."

"And if I'm good, it'll pay?"

He nodded. "If you're good enough."

For a long moment, I sat and struggled with the thought of going back to a gym and wondered how I'd feel once I was inside the ring. I stole another glance at Ethan and decided all that mattered was that I got another chance to see him – hopefully one with his shirt off, covered in sweat, and in a fight with someone.

I had an excuse to take another glance. So I did. "Do you train there?"

"Sure do."

He didn't talk much, but when he did, he didn't have the Texas thing going on with his voice. I wondered where he was from. I decided Los Angeles. An actor turned boxer. The more I studied his handsome face, the more I was sure of it. A displaced actor.

I'd made my decision. I glanced at Ripp. "When do we start?"

He shrugged. "Be there tomorrow at noon?"

The thought of seeing Ethan again caused me to smile. I let Ripp believe it was him training me that caused my expression of delight.

"Sounds good," I said.

And it did.

It sounded really good.

TWO

JAZ

Day two.

As soon as I walked in, I was met by the smell of sweat, adrenaline, broken noses and broken dreams. Memories of my old gym came rushing back, sending a tingling sensation the length of my spine. What little reservation I had about training instantly vanished, and I quickly filled with a desire to once again enter the ring.

My eyes darted around the massive room. There were at least a dozen rings, all filled with boxers and surrounded by on-lookers. I stood quietly by the entrance and surveyed the entire area. Disappointed that I didn't immediately see Ethan, my eyes soon found a familiar face. As he approached, I couldn't help but smile.

"This place is huge."

"Biggest in Austin," Ripp said. He nodded toward my empty hands. "Where's your gear?"

"Well, that's something I was going to talk to you about. I don't really have any."

"What have you been using?"

"I uhhm. I haven't been to a gym since I was sixteen."

He looked confused. "You ain't been to a gym since you were sixteen? That uppercut you swung looked pretty polished. So did that hook into his ribs."

I grinned.

"So you need some gear?" he asked.

Dressed in a sports bra, a sleeveless tee, and a pair of shorts, all I really needed was some shoes and a pair of training gloves to get into the ring. I had neither. I felt embarrassed. My eyes feel to the floor.

"Follow me," he said.

In what was probably a walking pace for him, but a shallow jog for me, he took off across the gym. I fought to catch up, but eventually did. I followed him outside of the gym, down a hallway, and into a small sporting goods store inside the far end of the building.

He pressed his hands against his hips and turned toward me. "Can you afford to buy gear right now?"

I pursed my lips and inhaled a shallow breath. I had a job as a waitress, but it wasn't a good one. While I prepared to respond, he reached down and gripped my wrist lightly in his hand. He dragged me through the store to the back corner, where the shoes were on display.

"Got some of the new Nike HyperKO's in a bunch of different colors. What color you like?" he asked.

"I uhhm. I like purple, but I can't really…"

He released my wrist, did the hands on the hips thing again, and cocked an eyebrow. "Grab some shoes and training gloves. I wanna see you in the ring."

"But I can't…"

He shook his head. "Let's just say I'm in tight with the owner. Grab what you want, and we'll work it out later. You know who owns this gym?"

I shrugged. "Who?"

He grinned his cheesy grin. "Good friend of mine." He chuckled. "Now pick out some fuckin' shoes."

Maybe he did, and maybe he didn't, but for some reason, I felt like he believed in me. I wasn't the type of person that lacked self-esteem or needed praise to feel like I was accomplishing my goals in life, but feeling like he had faith in my ability to box was reassuring.

I did as he asked and picked out some new shoes, a pair of training gloves, and some glove wraps. After jumping rope and spending some time on the speed bag, we climbed into an empty ring. I felt guilty for thinking Ripp was a big meathead when we met. Dressed in shorts, a wife beater, boxing shoes, and with the mitts on his hands, he looked like a trainer, not a gym rat.

"I just want to see your form. No need to try and impress me, just react to what I tell ya. Ready?"

I nodded.

He held the mitts in front of his chest. It had been years since I'd trained, but when I was sixteen, I had more talent than most of the people at the gym, regardless of their age, sex, or experience. No one needed to tell me, I could see it for myself. My trainer reminded me of it daily, nonetheless.

"Right jab."

I thrust my right hand into the mitt.

"Again."

I hit it again.

"Two more."

I jabbed again, twice.

He grinned and nodded.

"Right. Again. Left hook."

I jabbed the mitt twice, and swung a left into Ripp's left mitt. With each command he gave, I followed with the instructed punch. His commands came quicker. So did my reaction.

"Left, right."

"Left, right, left, left. Left, left. Right."

"Hook to the body."

"Hook to the head."

"Left. Again. Again. Two more. Again. Again," he barked. "Right hand. Another. Left, Right. Left. Left. Hook the body. Hook the head."

After the last punch, he lowered the mitts and stood up straight. "You ain't been in a gym since you was sixteen?"

I shook my head.

His eyes narrowed. "Bullshit."

"It's not, I swear. I mean, I've always worked out, but I haven't been to a gym and trained."

"Who trained you when you were a kid?"

"An old man at the gym. Freddy Lewis," I said. "He died right after my sixteenth birthday."

"I'm sorry," he said, his tone of voice convincing me he meant every word he said. "That's when you quit trainin'?"

That was when everything in my life changed, but all of that didn't matter much. I didn't really want to talk about it, so I simply shrugged.

He straightened his stance and locked eyes with me. "I ain't here for the fame or the money," he said. "I'm here because fightin' is part of who I am. I've tried to walk away from it more than once, but I can't. As far as bein' a trainer goes, I sure ain't the best, but I can train you to be *your* best. You ain't no amateur, Jaz. Not even close. I can see that already. So, you gonna let me train ya?"

I nodded eagerly.

"You wanna spar with someone? Just some light stuff? I'd like to see your form."

I raised my gloves and tapped them together. "I'm ready."

"Loosen up," he said. "Lemme see what I can come up with."

He ducked under the ropes, stomped across the gym, and disappeared into the crowd of people. A few minutes later, he returned. Fitted with gloves and carrying headgear, he grinned his cheesy grin and stepped into the ring.

"Ain't got a girl for you to spar with and none of the men want to step in with ya." He said. "Let's get this headgear on ya and you can spar with me."

I seemed foolish for him not to wear headgear. But, like everyone else, he believed a girl couldn't threaten a man.

He was wrong.

"You're not going to wear head gear?"

He shook his head. "Don't worry. You ain't gonna hurt me. Only been down once, and that came from the heavyweight Champion of the World."

"No shit?"

He pressed the headgear over my head. "No shit."

Impressive.

Easily standing eight inches taller than me, he bent his knees, lowered his shoulders, and raised his gloves. We made eye contact.

He nodded. "Bring it."

He threw a few slow jabs in my direction, pulling his punches before they made contact. With my chin tucked and my gloves protecting my face, I bobbed from side-to-side, easily avoiding each punch.

17

His speed and intensity increased.

I continued to escape most of his attempts with head movements alone, blocking a few of the more powerful punches with my gloves. His efforts were slight and short, and I had yet to even throw a single punch at him.

He leaned back slightly. "I want all you got, okay?"

"You sure?"

"Yep."

I tapped my gloves against his. "Tell me when."

He nodded.

From what I had seen, he typically held his left hand a few inches lower than his right. I lowered my right glove, giving him a reason to extend his left arm. When he did, I threw a right jab past his lowered left glove and toward his chin.

The punch connected well. I knew it didn't hurt him, but he was clearly shocked. When he reacted to being hit, I threw a quick – but powerless – left hook to his ribs. As he lowered his right elbow in reaction to the punch, I threw a right-left combo at his head, connecting both punches.

Didn't think I had it in me, did you?

He said he wanted it all, and I intended to give it to him.

He pushed me off and raised his gloves. I unleashed a barrage of punches into his exposed ribs, causing him to lower his hands again. When they came down, I pounded him with a hard right cross.

The punch made him stumble.

Surprised?

I tucked my elbows to my sides, lowered my chin, and stepped toward him, bringing a left hook followed by a right uppercut with me.

Both punches connected hard, and in response, he signaled for me to stop. A gravelly voice from beside us caused me to shift my focus to the side of the ring.

"What in the name of God almighty is going on here?"

"Light sparrin'," Ripp responded.

An older man – roughly seventy by my guess – stood outside the ring with his arms folded in front of his chest. He glanced at me, looked at Ripp, and shook his head. "Don't look light to me," he growled. "Looks to me like she was whippin' your ass."

"This is Jaz, Old Man. I'm thinkin' I'm gonna train her," Ripp said.

I raised my gloves and nodded my head toward the old man. He made eye contact and held my gaze for a moment. Then, he turned toward Ripp and glared. Ripp tossed his hands in the air, and the old man walked away without speaking.

"Is he mad?" I asked.

"He ain't mad, he's just old."

"Is he the one who owns the place?"

"No. Just kind of runs it. His name's Kelsey. He's always in a bad fuckin' mood. But, he trained the current Heavyweight Champion, so I guess he can be however he wants."

"No shit?"

"No shit."

I'd been out of the sport so long, I didn't even know who the champion was. I raised my gloves as if I were ready to box. "So, what did you think?"

"About you?"

I nodded.

"I ain't tryin' to inflate your ego, but you got skills."

"Mad skills?"

He looked at me like I had three eyes. "What the fuck does that mean?"

"Am I a bad ass?" I asked jokingly.

"You're pretty close," he said.

I swelled with pride.

He cocked an eyebrow. "What do you want out of this?"

I didn't have to think long to give my response. "On the sign outside, it says 'we train champions'. That's what I want. I want to be the champion."

"Never made it myself. So you're my only fuckin' hope at a title." He swung his glove against my shoulder, knocking me off balance with the punch.

I regained my footing and grinned. "I'll try not to let you down."

"Let me down?" He shook his head. "You're too fuckin' good, Jaz."

"You really think so?"

"Know so."

It had been almost ten years since I stepped foot in a ring, and equally as long since I'd fought anyone. At that moment, however, I felt like I could have defeated anyone, regardless of their size, ability, experience, or training.

And only time would tell if I was right or wrong.

THREE

JAZ

Day nine.

While working out on the heavy bag, I noticed him come through the door. He looked no differently than he did the day we met.

Like a disciplined athlete.

He walked right past me. Either he didn't notice me or he didn't care. Whichever it was, I wasn't willing to accept it.

I turned toward him and admired his cute ass for a few strides before I spoke. "Are you always such a dick?" I asked as he walked past.

He continued to walk away without so much as acknowledging what I had said.

"Ethan," I shouted.

He paused and glanced over his shoulder. "Yes?"

"Are you always such a dick?"

"No," he responded.

And he walked away.

What the fuck?

I had been training for a week, and hadn't seen Ethan once. After learning he worked out in the late afternoons, I decided to extend my schedule in hope of seeing him. As I watched him begin to jump rope, I couldn't help but wonder if he was just an asshole.

21

A really hot asshole.

As much as I wanted to get to know him, I wasn't about to let his attitude have an effect on my training. I pounded two and three-punch combinations into the bag, glancing toward him every chance I got. The thirty-minute workout was over before I knew it. He didn't look in my direction once. I didn't want to be disappointed that he paid no attention to me, but I was.

I couldn't help but wonder if he was in a relationship, gay, or just not interested. I hoped he wasn't interested, because it was something I felt I could at least attempt to resolve. If he was gay or in a relationship, I realized I'd simply have to accept him as being off-limits.

I finished my workout and put up my gloves. No matter how desperately I wanted to get to know Ethan, I wasn't about to make him feel like I was chasing him. Encouraging him, however, was a different story. I pulled my sleeveless tee off and stuffed it in the bag. Now dressed in nothing but shorts and a sports bra, I shouldered my bag and walked toward the locker room.

I'd never been a pretentious or conceited woman, but I was well aware that I was attractive. I was in great physical shape, my ass was cute, and my tits were fantastic. I wouldn't argue that my hair needed to be cut, but pulled into a ponytail, it looked as good as anyone else's.

And I had it in a ponytail.

I strutted past Ethan and toward the far end of the gym, doing my best to look irresistible. Fighting the urge not to turn around, I walked into the locker room, looked in the mirror, and exhaled. I looked great. How could he not see it? I got undressed and took a shower, wondering the entire time if he'd noticed me, and if he did, what he was thinking.

Being fascinated by someone and having them show no interest in return isn't an easy thing for a woman to accept, and I wasn't much different than anyone else in that respect. Wondering what it was about me that he didn't like, I got dressed and left the locker room.

I walked past him again, poking my earbuds in my ears as I passed by. When I was almost to the door, I could see his reflection in the glass.

"I wasn't trying to be an asshole," he said.

I didn't even have my iPod turned on and had heard him just fine, but I didn't want him to know it. I pulled my right earbud out, turned around, and shot him a false look of surprise. "Did you say something?"

He was so attractive it made me nervous to stand there looking at him. Turning away wasn't really an option, though.

"I said I wasn't trying to be an asshole."

I draped the earbud over my shoulder. "Just comes natural for you?"

His eyes fell to the floor for a few seconds. After a light sigh, he looked up. "You're intimidating."

What? Me?

I was shocked. And this time it wasn't a show. "Me? How would I be intimidating to *you*?"

"Don't act like you don't know you're gorgeous," he said. "And. Well. After seeing what you did to that guy at Starbucks, it's pretty obvious you're a much better fighter than I'll ever be."

I stood and gawked at him, partially because he was so fucking handsome, and in part because of the compliments he had just given me. I was flattered. "I don't know about all that, but thank you" I said. "And don't worry, I won't bite. I mean, not unless you want me to."

He looked embarrassed. As always, I came off a little too strong. It was one of my strengths – or weaknesses – depending on how one looked at it. He grinned nonetheless. "So, Ripp said he's going to train you."

"Yeah. Looks that way. Does he train you?"

He shook his head. "No. One of the other guys here does."

"Oh," I said.

I wondered where Ripp ranked in comparison to the other trainers, and hoped I made the right choice regarding having him train me. "So, how does Ripp compare to the other guys as far as training goes?"

He widened his eyes and chuckled. "As far as the other guys go, there's no comparison. Kelsey's first and Ripp's second. But Kelsey doesn't train anyone but Dekk."

"Who's Dekk?"

"Seriously?"

"Yeah." I shrugged. "I don't know anyone yet."

He waved his arms toward the open facility. "Dekk. He owns the place. He's the Heavyweight Champion of the World. Shane Dekkar's his real name. Kelsey trains him. He's best friends with Ripp."

"Ripp said he was friends with the owner. I guess that explains it."

"I can't believe you didn't know who he was."

"I haven't followed the sport since I was sixteen," I said, feeling slightly foolish for not knowing. "I know now, though."

He grinned and nodded. "I'll point him out when he comes in."

At that moment, I really didn't care who the champion was, who owned the gym, or how well-connected Ripp was with him. I wanted to get to know Ethan. "So, are you done for the night?"

I doubted he was, because he hadn't done much in the thirty minutes since he'd arrived – at least not as far as I was concerned. Prepared for him to explain how he needed to spend another hour and a half at the gym, and for him to give a lengthy excuse on why he couldn't take time to see me more, I waited for his response.

"Yeah," he said, looking toward the station where he'd been working out "I think I'm done."

So, you wanna fuck?

I fought the urge to be myself and stuck with something a little less invasive to his seemingly shy personality. "So, you want to go get a coffee or something?"

"Sure."

Wow. That was easy.

"You need to shower?"

He looked like he considered it for a nanosecond, then shook his head. "Didn't really sweat."

"Grab your stuff. We can go talk or whatever."

I was hoping for some *whatever*, but was prepared to settle for getting to know him a little better. In a moment he returned with his bag and we walked to the parking lot together.

"You want to ride with me?" he asked.

"Sure."

He opened the passenger door to a truck that was parked right beside the door. I had been on several dates, and I couldn't recall anyone ever opening the door for me, regardless of who they were. As I hoisted myself into the truck, I couldn't help but feel like we were going out for the evening.

He carefully closed the door and then climbed in the other side.

"So, where are you from?" I asked.

"Born and raised in Texas. Grew up in Lubbock."

Most born and raised southern boys were extremely polite. My belief that he was shy and reserved was probably nothing but him being mannerly.

"You don't sound like you're from here."

"What do you mean?"

"You don't have the southern accent thing going on."

"My parents were originally from Chicago. They didn't speak with an accent, and they thought if we did it would make us sound uneducated. We had to take speech classes when we were kids so we didn't *sound like idiots*."

"Seriously?"

"Dead serious." He chuckled. "My father's a hard ass."

I knew all there was to know about having a father who was difficult but wasn't prepared to discuss it. At least not yet.

"What about you?" he asked.

"Omaha, Nebraska. I was on my way to the beach and ended up here. Been here ever since."

He steered the truck into the other lane, and then looked at me. One of his eyebrows raised slightly. Not much, but just enough to express his interest. "You were on your way to the beach?"

It still thrilled me to think that one day I would see it. Feel the wet sand between my toes. Feel the waves against my skin. "Yeah. I've never been. So, after high school I headed that direction. But, I only got this far."

"The bad thing about seeing the ocean is that it's hard to leave," he said, his voice trailing off as if his mind was searching for fading memories. "There's something about it…"

My eyes went wide. "You've been?"

He nodded. "When I was a kid. And then on spring break. It's…it's awesome."

"I'm going," I said. "As soon as I can afford it."

I felt more comfortable with him now that we were just talking like two old friends. He was still extremely good-looking – and intimidatingly so – but his demeanor made me feel like he had no idea how handsome he really was. As he pulled into the parking lot of the coffee shop, my curiosity got the best of me.

"So, are you single?"

He parked the truck and then his eyes searched my face. After a moment, he seemed to find whatever he was searching for. "Yeah."

His hesitation made me feel like he was either lying or hiding something. I pressed a little further. "Are you sure?"

"Positive. It's just…"

"Just what?"

"My last relationship ended kind of...I don't know…it just. It was kind of," he stammered. "I wasn't ready for it to, and it just ended."

He couldn't say something like that and not expect me to pry a little further. So, pry I did. "What happened? I mean, if I can ask. I had a pretty bad one too, and believe me, that fucker just ended. From great to gone in one day. It sucks, but life just kind of sucks sometimes."

"I don't think life sucks. I think things happen. Things that are out of our control."

Now he had my complete interest. "So are you going to tell me what happened?"

He gripped the steering wheel and stared straight ahead, out into the street. I waited for him to drop the bomb, expecting something totally insane. Expecting a story of how he caught his girlfriend with one of his friends, or that she gave him some weird STD, I sat quietly and waited. While I formulated my response in advance for whatever it was he was

27

going to tell me, he closed his eyes and let out a sigh.

He opened his eyes but didn't look at me. "She uhhm. She was getting gas. And some guy came out of the gas station and just started shooting. He'd robbed the place. They said the bullet ricocheted off the pavement. It. It uhhm. It hit…"

He tapped his temple with the tip of his finger.

Openmouthed and speechless, I sat and stared. My stomach turned. I felt sick, and I wished I hadn't pried. I wondered if she was paralyzed or had died, but there was no way I could ask, even if I felt I wanted to.

"We'd uhhm. I used to smoke, and she hated it. We'd been in a fight about it. She told me to quit, or else." He coughed out a dry laugh that quickly got emotional. "I uhhm. I never cared much for someone giving me an ultimatum, so I told her I'd quit when I was ready. She left, and it was the last time I saw her alive."

I stared down at my bag, not really knowing what to say. I tried to swallow, but my dry mouth prevented it. A long silence followed. It wasn't a tremendous amount of time, but it was enough that I grew uncomfortable and filled with guilt.

"You know," he said. "I wonder about things. Like if I would have agreed to quit, she never would have got mad and left. If that would have happened, she'd be alive, you know."

His thoughts must have weighed heavily on him, because he paused for what seemed like an eternity before he continued. "If I wouldn't have been so stubborn, I wonder if things might have been different. Eventually, I always seem to remember what the pastor said in church when I was a kid about this world being God's world, and not ours. And then I think that for whatever reason, God decided it was just her time."

He looked right at me. "Either way, it sucks."

Sometimes I wished I could just haul off and kick life right in the balls. He was right, it sucked. I was glad he told me the story, but felt terrible for all but forcing him to do so.

"You're right," I managed to say. "It does suck. And, I'm sorry."

Saying I was sorry seemed shallow and simple, but I didn't know what else to say. I wanted to console him, but knew there was really nothing I could do or say to provide him with any degree of comfort beyond what he already felt.

I decided to try anyway. His eyes seemed distant and sad, which didn't surprise me at all.

"You quit smoking, right?"

He held my gaze. "Yeah."

"I bet wherever she is, she's proud of you."

It wasn't much, but it was all I could come up with.

His eyes narrowed. He appeared to be considering what I said. After a moment he shifted his focus to the street. Then, he chuckled. It seemed strange to hear him laugh, but I accepted it as being better than a lot of things he could have done.

"I never looked at it that way," he said. "I like that. Thank you."

I decided at least for the time being that silence ruled, so I simply smiled and chose not to speak.

He smiled in return.

On that night, his laughter and his smile satisfied me so deeply that I believed moving to Austin was for that reason and that reason alone.

FOUR

JAZ

Day fourteen.

My mind drifted to thoughts of many things the instant I saw Ethan – all of which included his cock. I had an unmistakable sexual attraction to him, and his lack of expressed interest in me only seemed to make matters worse.

Backing down in the ring – or in life – wasn't an option. I had always fought for what I believed in, and I believed we needed to be fucking.

It wasn't any one characteristic that attracted me to him, it was everything. Each individual thing about him made him attractive, but everything combined made me long for him sexually. I didn't want him to fuck me to simply satisfy a sexual void, it was more of a desire to have him claim me.

So I could claim him in return.

He ran his fingers through his perfectly fucked up hair. It was going in every available direction, like it always did. It was brown, short, and permanently uncombed, but undeniably sexy. Bedroom hair. He had bedroom hair. I tried not to stare and made a point to make sure my mouth wasn't hanging open.

He leaned into the back of the booth and pushed his uneaten food to the side. I glanced at his plate. Half of his hamburger stared back at me, taunting me to eat it.

I eyed the burger. Pieces of bacon jutted out from between the bun and the thick patty of meat. "You're not going to finish it?"

"I'm full," he said, his tone of voice expressing his lack of interest in finishing the meal. "Do you want it?"

He must have seen the hunger in my eyes.

"I don't *want* it," I lied. "But I'd hate to see it go to waste."

He pushed the plate toward me. "Here."

"You sure you don't want it?"

"I'm not that hungry."

I shrugged as if it was no big deal, and that I was simply making my contribution to minimize the food waste that hindered the city's sanitary engineering department. A few seconds later, and the burger was gone.

He grinned and nodded his head in my direction. "You eat a lot."

I didn't live on a *limited* budget. With my shitty waitress job, I would describe it as more of an ongoing economic strain. I couldn't buy gas for my car, pay my rent, *and* eat, so I often had to decide if driving or eating was more important. I typically chose to shoulder my backpack and walk, which made me even hungrier.

More often than not I felt like I was losing the battle, and lately it seemed to be much worse. Although I had always exercised, the addition of my boxing training to my typical daily routine had me needing to consume far more calories than what I was used to. My income, however, prevented me from the luxury of doing so. I needed to win the lottery, but spending the money on a ticket wasn't necessarily in my budget.

I wiped the corners of my mouth and took a drink of water. "I'm burning up all my calories in the gym."

"How long are your workouts?"

"I've been going for three hours a day."

"Three hours?"

I nodded. "Yeah. Maybe I'm making up for lost time."

Considering how rewarding I found the sport to be, it struck me as odd that I had spent so much time away from the gym.

"How long has it been since you boxed, again?"

"Eight years," I said, although I wasn't really sure.

"Why'd you stop?"

It was a good question. I didn't want to, but at the time, I felt I had no real alternative.

"My trainer got cancer," I said. "And he died. Like almost immediately."

The look on his face did little to hide his guilt. "I'm sorry."

"It's not your fault. It was just one of those things. Part of life." I shrugged. "He hated the doctor, so he never went. Ended up getting colon cancer. If he would have gone in for one of those scope things they probably would have caught it. But, by the time they found out, it was too late."

"And you couldn't find another trainer?"

My father hated the fact that I chose boxing as my sport of interest, but I did it primarily to stay away from him and his abusive behavior. He'd wanted a boy, and was forced to accept me as his only child, as my mother died of complications while giving birth. Initially, I felt my involvement in the sport would make him proud, but he never once expressed it.

Freddy stepped into my life as a trainer, but ended up playing the part of a mentor and a fatherly figure both. During years I trained at the gym, my father's harsh physical abuse slowed considerably, but never stopped. I suspected he feared Freddy's retribution and I even wondered if he had threatened my father at some point. When he died, my dreams of being a professional boxer – and of escaping my father's abuse – vanished.

Accepting the death of a man as close to me as Freddy when I was sixteen was something that took time. He treated me like a daughter, and his eyes filled with excitement when he spoke to me or about me – similar to the way Ripp's eyes looked after he saw me beat the guy at the coffee shop.

I never sought out another trainer, and my way of dealing with my father's abuse changed from going to the gym to leaving home as soon as school was over.

"I could have," I said. "I guess I just didn't want to at the time."

"What made you decide to now?"

My response came easy, and seemed simple as a result. "I liked the way Ripp seemed excited when he talked about my mad skills. He reminded me of Freddy."

He smiled and nodded, although I doubted he fully understood my attachment to men who acted like Ripp. The hole my father left in my life was something I felt a need to fill, and men like Freddy and Ripp filled it – and did so very well.

I stared at the miscellaneous uneaten garnishments on Ethan's plate. Not because I wanted to eat them, but because focusing on them prevented me from staring at Ethan.

"I think I fight to get rid of my anger," he said.

He seemed so peaceful and kind. In fact, I attributed his lackluster performance in the ring to the absence of anger. "What anger?"

"My father," he responded. "He was an asshole. *Is* an asshole. I mean, he still is. I just don't see him much anymore."

I shrugged. "Mine too."

He leaned forward and looked right at me. "Mine was really demanding, and he'd whip us for no reason. Sometimes I thought he did it just because he enjoyed it."

"Trade ya," I said.

He leaned away from the table and returned a confused look. "Huh?"

"Trade mine for yours. Mine used to beat me with his fists. When I got older, I'd hit him back. It made me feel better, but it just made him hit me harder."

"He hit you? Like…" He clenched his fist and raised it in the air. "With his fist?"

It wasn't something I typically told people. And, as terrible as it sounded, it was true. True and disturbing. I nodded. "Yeah."

"Holy crap." His eyes fell to the table. For some time, it seemed he was trying to think of something to say, but he didn't speak.

Thinking about what my father had done to me, I sat silently while my hatred toward him grew. There was a long list of things he could have chosen to do that I would have been able to forgive him for, but beating me from the time I was a toddler until I decided to leave wasn't one of them.

After a very long – and rather awkward – silence, Ethan looked up. His eyes were red and seemed swollen. "I don't even know what to say."

I stared back at him and forced a smile.

You already said it.

FIVE

JAZ

Day seventeen.

According to Ripp, I was far too advanced to continue in the amateur circuit, but Kelsey didn't seem to agree.

So, roughly two weeks into my training, an amateur fight was set up between me and a girl from Dallas. She had only fought in the amateurs, but so far she was undefeated. I wasn't worried, because although I hadn't boxed since I was sixteen, I was still undefeated.

"Throw those jabs like I taught ya. Find out what her technique is, and look for an opening."

I pressed my gloves into the side of my headgear and nodded.

"You good?"

I pounded my gloves together. "Mmhhmm."

He cleared his throat. "Listen to me, Jaz."

We locked eyes.

"Remember this, tonight and always," he said. "Fear will get you hurt and arrogance will get you knocked the fuck out. But confidence? Confidence will get you keep you in the game."

It was great advice. I nodded.

He turned and nodded toward the ring attendant. I glanced at Ethan, who was standing beside the ring with a few other people I didn't know.

I raised my gloves and mentally smiled as we made eye contact.

He smiled in return.

The referee stepped to the center of the ring. Linda 'Left Hook' Lopez and I followed. Although he gave no fight instructions, he made us touch gloves. We stepped a few feet from each other and glared.

The bell rang, signaling the start of the fight.

She immediately rushed toward me, which was fine for my fighting style. I'd always felt I was a diverse fighter, and was equally as comfortable fighting offensively as I was defensively.

She swung a well telegraphed left hook, opening up her right side. I'd been taught by Freddy to give an opponent some time to expose her strengths and weaknesses before I went in for the kill, and Ripp reiterated the same advice.

I leaned away from the punch, and it swung past me. After a few light jabs on both of our parts, she swung the same slow left hook. I blocked the punch and looked at the gaping hole she left me to counterpunch through.

Sorry, Ripp, but she's asking for it.

I tucked my chin into my chest and responded with a straight right cross before she recovered from the punch she'd thrown. The punch, probably one of my most powerful, landed directly on her chin.

Her legs went wobbly and her hands dropped.

Hurts like a motherfucker, huh?

I felt like I could have ended the fight right then and there, but I wanted whoever was watching to see everything I was capable of.

A left hook to her ribs caused her eyes to go wide, and she looked like she would have forfeited the fight if she would have been asked.

The problem, at least for her, was that no one was asking.

And I was still hoping to impress whoever was watching.

I followed up with a lightning-fast four punch combination, connecting each one right in the middle of her face.

It was thirty seconds into the fight, and she hadn't hit me once. I, on the other hand, had connected six powerful punches, and she was in trouble. I stepped back in hope of her coming to me for a little more. She teetered on legs that didn't want to continue and feet that had other plans.

She looked like she was planning on leaving.

Just remember, this is only business.

I knew she'd be expecting my left hook, so I threw it. Slow and without much strength, I didn't throw it to hurt her – or to even hit her for that matter. It was more to get her to open up for my right. Having been hit by my left hand twice – and not wanting it again – she twisted her upper body to the left, undoubtedly hoping the punch would glance off of her torso.

It was exactly what I wanted. With her facing to the left, and open to my right hand, I fed it to her.

Hard.

The punch caught the left side of her jaw. Her feet came up and she fell to the mat like someone had dropped her out of an airplane.

The ref stepped between us and waved his hands over her, signaling the end of the fight.

Excited, I glanced toward my corner. Ripp's hands were held high over his head, and the expression on his face did nothing to hide his pride.

The old man, Kelsey, was standing at his side.

I rushed to the corner, proud of my accomplishment. Ripp removed my headgear and pulled my mouthpiece. "So much for using the jab to establish your opponent's fuckin' technique, huh?"

"Sorry, Boss. She was asking for it."

The old man glared at me. His face was weathered, his hair was thin, and he had on the same old-school satin jacket he was wearing the first time I had seen him. He looked angry and tired. "Lift your right heel. You're fightin' flat footed," he said dryly.

I started to thank him for the constructive criticism, and figured I'd let the condescending tone of his voice slide, but he turned around before I could say anything. I arched an eyebrow in his direction as he sauntered away.

"Don't worry about him," Ripp said.

I didn't want it to, but it bothered me that Kelsey didn't seem to like me. I shook it off and fixed my excited eyes on Ripp. "How'd I look?"

"You looked like a champion," he said, his voice filled with excitement. He lowered his tone to a more demanding one and motioned with his eyes toward the other corner of the ring. "Now act like one."

I shot him a confused stare.

"Go tell that girl she fought a good fight."

I rushed to the far corner, congratulated my opponent, and climbed out of the ring. Ethan and Ripp stood off to the side talking. I felt like I was on top of the world and wanted to share my joy with anyone who cared to listen, but the first thing I needed to do was eat.

"I haven't eaten anything but a protein bar since 3:00. I'm starving," I said. "If you guys want to come over to my apartment, we can celebrate. I'll make some chicken."

"Chicken? Women after my own fuckin' heart right there," Ripp said, slapping his hand against Ethan's shoulder. "How 'bout we all go out to eat and celebrate? I'm buying."

"I can cook," I assured him.

"You beat that girl like she stole somethin' from ya." Ripp chuckled. "We need to go out and celebrate."

If the severity of the beatings I gave my opponents assured me a free meal after each fight, I'd beat the brakes off of every girl who stepped in the ring with me. I remembered what Ripp said about arrogance, however, and dropped my gaze to the floor. "I got in a couple of lucky punches."

"Lucky punches my ass." He tossed his head toward the locker room. "Go wash the stink off your ass so we can go."

Ethan had remained quiet since the end of the fight, and I couldn't help but wonder if he felt somewhat jealous about my win. His amateur record wasn't terrible, but it wasn't fantastic either. Six wins and seven losses wasn't anything to be ashamed of, but it wasn't a record a typical fighter would brag about, either.

I glanced at Ethan. "Are you going to go?"

Ripp slapped his hand against Ethan's shoulder. "Fuck yeah he's goin'."

Ethan nodded and smiled a shallow smile. "You looked great. And yeah, if you want me to, I'll go."

"If I want you to?" I shot him a look. "If you don't go, maybe I'll give you some of what I gave her."

His eyes went wide and he chuckled, although I could tell he was just being theatrical. "Fighting with you? I might like that."

The thought of fighting and fucking at the same time made my pussy tingle. I tried to refrain from being my natural self and making a sexual comment, especially in front of Ripp. I kept my response simple, but somewhat expressive of my thoughts on the subject.

"Not near as much as I would," I said with a wink of my eye.

And I walked away.

SIX

JAZ

Day seventeen.

"No, it wasn't over a piece of fuckin' ass. And it damned sure wasn't in the parking lot of the old gym," Ripp complained. "God damned rumors. I'll tell you how the deal went down if you'll just sit still for a fuckin' minute, you nervous actin' fucker."

Sitting on the other side of the booth, across from Ethan and me, Ripp was telling the story of how he met the heavyweight boxing champion. I pressed my right hand against Ethan's chest as if to eliminate him from the conversation, and made eye contact with Ripp. "I don't care if *he* wants to hear it or not. I do. So tell me."

He leaned forward and playfully arched an eyebrow. "We'll need a refill. This'll take a minute."

I raised my hand and got the attention of our waitress. "Another round, please."

She smiled and nodded.

Ripp drank what was left of his beer and slid the empty bottle to the side. "So, they told me this undefeated boxer was comin' in from Compton, California. And I'm thinkin' he's gonna be some surfer dude. You know, long hair, all tan from playin' on the beach, and that he'd be wearin' flip flops and one a them fuckin' wet suits."

He gazed beyond me as if he was recalling the night in question, grinned, and shook his head. "Well, that wasn't the deal at all. This fucker rides his Harley from Compton to Austin, non-stop. 1,380 fuckin' miles with all of his shit tied on the back. I'm tellin' ya. And he hops off that bitch at about eight o'clock at night, just about the time ol' Ripp's gettin' ready to go out and knock off a piece of ass. He's wearing raggedy-assed boots with his socks showin' through all the holes in 'em, a hoodie, and a pair of faded Levi's. Weird fucker sure as fuck didn't look like a boxer."

His eyes went wide and he leaned forward, exchanging glances between Ethan and me. "Now, just so you know, this was back when Lightnin' Wilson was givin' me pointers on cage fightin', and he'd been trainin' me on that very night. So, Ol' Lightnin' comes up and says, 'Hey, that kid from Compton's here. You want to go four rounds with him?' Hell, I thought it was gonna be a walk in the park. But it sure as fuck wasn't."

He leaned back, folded his massive arms in front of his chest, and shook his head.

"What happened?" I asked excitedly.

I couldn't imagine anyone wanting to fight Ripp. He was probably 6'-4", weighed about 240 pounds, and was nothing but solid muscle. His in-your-face personality and general bad boy appearance were equally as intimidating as his size, and should act as a deterrent to anyone dumb enough to consider stepping in the ring with him.

He picked up his empty beer bottle by the neck and wagged it back and forth like a pendulum. "I can't talk unless I got a beer in my hand."

Luckily, the waitress dropped off our drinks – Michelob Ultra for Ripp and Ethan, and water for me. Ripp drank half the bottle of beer in one gulp, then continued his story.

"So, I told Ol' Lightnin' that I'd fight this California fool, and I figured it'd be over in about five minutes, because it was gonna take me three to lace up my gloves."

He twisted his mouth to the side, cocked one eyebrow, and made eye contact with Ethan, and then me. "So, three to lace up my gloves, and I was givin' this Compton cock sucker two minutes in the ring with me. Back then, they called me *The Ripper.* You know why?"

Engrossed in the story, I didn't respond with anything more than simply shaking my head.

"I ripped the heads off every fucker that came in the ring. I was undefeated. Never knocked out, and never knocked to the mat. Not even once."

I glanced at Ethan. He was as engrossed in the story as I was. I turned back to Ripp and grinned.

"So," he said. "Ol' California steps in the ring, and we touch 'em up. Now I'm thinking I'm gonna feed this prick a three piece, let him stagger around a minute, and then I'll finish him off. Now, remember, he probably hadn't showered in twenty-four hours, and he'd rode that damned Harley halfway across the US of A in a hundred-degree heat. So, this fucker smelled like rotten leather and fucking gasoline and I wasn't tryin' to smell him for too damned long. So, the bell rings, and I meet this fucker in the center of the ring. He's got his left hangin' a little low, and his right cocked like he's gonna feed it to me, so I stick him with a quick jab just to let him know how we do it here in Texas."

He coughed out a laugh and shook his head. I anxiously waited for him to continue, but he reached for his beer and took a drink instead. After what seemed like an eternity, I asked the inevitable.

"What happened?"

He took another drink and shrugged. "Don't know."

"What do you mean you don't know?"

"I don't know what happened, all I know is what Kelsey and Joe told me. Well, them and Lightnin'."

"What'd they tell you?"

"Told me the kid hit me with a left hook, followed it up with a right cross, and then what I learned was his signature punch."

I swallowed hard at the thought of Ripp being beaten. I reduced my voice to a whisper. "What was it?"

He fixed his eyes on me and arched one eyebrow. "Left uppercut."

"And he knocked you out?"

He nodded. "Knocked me out cold. Shit, I was punch drunk for a week. Kid hits like a fuckin' mule kicks. Imagine lettin' a barnyard mule haul off and kick you in the skull. Well, that's what it feels like to have Ol' Shane Dekkar hit ya."

Holy crap.

"And now you're friends?"

He took a drink of beer and coughed out a laugh. "Friends? Hell, we're more like brothers. Ain't no secret, but Dekk's dad got killed in the war, and his mom left when he was a kid. So, my parent's all but adopted his turkey sandwich eatin' ass. Now he comes over to their house with his wife and kid every Sunday for dinner."

"That's awesome," I said.

He chuckled. "The gettin' knocked out part, or the adoptin' Dekk part?"

"Both," I said. "Getting knocked out let you guys become friends."

"It damned sure did." He shifted his eyes from me to Ethan. "Now

46

you know the truth. It wasn't over a piece of ass. And it wasn't a drunken parking lot brawl, either. Can't have rumors like that floatin' around."

"That's just what I heard," Ethan said with a shrug. "Thanks for clearing it up."

Ripp glanced at his watch. "Shit, I got to get out of here, or my wife's gonna have my ass." He reached for his wallet, pulled out two $100 bills, and tossed them on the table. "Pay the tab with that, and leave whatever's left for a tip."

He slapped his hand against the edge of the table as he stood up. "Good show tonight, Jaz." He glanced at Ethan. "Get your heart in the game, kid."

Ethan waved his hand toward Ripp as if dismissing his comment. "Go home."

As Ripp walked away, I turned to Ethan. "What did he mean by that? *Get your heart in the game?*"

Ethan rolled his eyes. "He always tells me my heart isn't in it. That's what we were talking about the day we met you at Starbucks."

"Is your heart in it?"

He shrugged. "Yeah, it is. But he gives me shit about my record. Too many losses. To him, it's all about winning. But I'm not in it for those reasons."

I returned a blank stare. *If you're not in it to win, why be in it at all?* "Why do you do it?"

"For me, boxing is kind of like an anger management thing, I guess. Sometimes I need to lose."

It didn't make sense to me, but I nodded nonetheless. "And losing satisfies you?"

"Sometimes I think it's exactly what I need. And sometimes I need to win. So, I go into the ring with different goals. Sometimes I go in with the understanding that I'm going to lose. Other times I go in with a desire to win."

It was an odd theory as far as I was concerned, but I found it interesting. A self-imposed punishment of sorts, I guessed. I needed to know more, so I pried a little further. "When you go in with the goal of winning, how many times have you lost?"

"None."

"And when you go in with the goal of losing?"

He grinned. "Lost them all."

"So, you're kind of undefeated." I laughed. "At least when you want to be."

"I guess that's one way to look at it."

"Have you told Ripp that you don't always want to win?"

"No." He shook his head. "I didn't want to get into it with him, so I just kept it to myself. I doubt he'd understand."

"I don't understand, but it's interesting."

"I don't *really* understand it," he said. "But I've got my theories."

"What are they?"

"There are times when I don't want to win, but I want to fight. I want to go in, fight, and lose. That's my plan, to lose. I think it's kind of like the kids in school who self-harmed themselves. It's a coping mechanism, or whatever. When I was a kid, I was expected to be perfect. It was pounded into my head, over and over. But, no one's perfect. I know that now, but I didn't know it then. Now, something inside of me tells me I need to be, but I'm smart enough to know I can't be. I think losing the fights help convince me that I'm in control. I know I *could* win, but I choose not to. Does that make sense?"

It was apparent Ethan's childhood wasn't much better than mine. I dealt with mine by leaving, physically separating myself from my father. He was attempting to deal with his by trying to be in control of something as uncontrollable as a fight.

"It does," I said.

The more I learned about him, the more I realized just how similar we were. I'd never spent a moment feeling sorry for myself, but I couldn't help but feel sorry for him.

"Anything else?" the waitress asked.

I looked at Ethan. He shook his head.

"No, thank you."

She placed the bill on the table. "Whenever you're ready, no rush."

I looked at the bill. It was only $102. I placed the two $100 bills in the check holder and folded it closed, feeling confident the waitress would be pleased with Ripp's $98 tip.

"Are you ready to go?"

"Sure."

I climbed out of the booth and extended my hand. He reached for it and smiled as I pulled against his weight, helping him slide from the booth. After he stood up, I continued to hold his hand in mine.

I walked toward the door with him at my side, completely expecting him to eventually release my hand or object in some way.

But it never came.

We walked to the truck hand-in-hand, and he opened the door for me, just like he did the night we went to the coffee shop. His manners, calm demeanor, and handsome good looks were proving to be just too much for me. It was at that moment, as I climbed inside the truck while he held the door, that I decided I wanted our friendship to go one step

49

further.

One very sexual step.

SEVEN

JAZ

Day twenty-four.

She looked at me like I was nothing shy of insane. "How old are you, again?"

"Twenty-four," I responded. "Why?"

"Because you're acting like you're fifteen."

"I am not," I huffed.

Our shifts had ended, and the diner was closed. We sat at a table in the center of the dining area talking about relationships and men. Not having had many close girlfriends over the years, I found value in Rachel, often asking her opinions about all things related to being a girl. We were roughly the same age, and she was really close to her mother, which made her advice seem almost motherly. This was, however, my first attempt to get advice from her about a man.

"You want to fuck him, right?"

It wasn't all I wanted, but it was part of it. I nodded, but felt the need to explain further. "I mean. Yeah. But not just *fuck* him. I want to--"

She waved her hands in the air jokingly. "Just stop. I don't want to hear it. You're talking to me because your head's in one place, and his is in another, right?"

"I suppose."

"You want him, and you're afraid he doesn't want you. Or he doesn't want you the same as you want him. Or whatever. Right?"

So far, on limited information, she sure seemed to understand the intricacies regarding my dilemma. Convinced I had made the right decision in confiding my relationship woes to her, I proceeded. "Right," I said. "It seems like he's moving along at one pace, and I'm at another."

"But. Your goal is to fuck him. You're each moving at a different pace, but the prize at the end of the race is sex, right?"

It sounded bad, but it was true. Kind of. I nodded in agreement. "I guess."

"This is so tenth grade. I swear," she said. "Tell him you want his dick."

As bold and as brash as I was, telling Ethan I wanted his cock seemed a bit overboard. I shot her a confused stare. "Just say it? 'Hey, Ethan, I want your cock?' I'm just supposed to tell him that? That's your *best* advice?"

She shrugged. "That's what I'd do."

In my experience, guys had always made the first move. I had never met anyone who was as uninterested in fucking me as Ethan, though. "Really?"

She chewed on her bottom lip and narrowed her eyes slightly. After a moment's thought, she released her lip and shook her head. "No, I'd probably suck his cock. No guy is going to deny you a blowjob. And what does a good blowjob lead to?"

I shrugged. "Sex?"

"Sex." She nodded and raised her index finger in the air. "As long as you don't let him finish. Don't forget that. You can't make him come. If you do, you'll just become that girl who sucks his dick, and you don't want that. Been there, done that. Not doing it again."

It sounded like utter nonsense. "Don't make him come?"

"God no. Just suck it long enough to drive him crazy. Then stop. He'll try and convince you to continue, but don't do it. Eventually, he'll give in. He'll fuck you. And, if for some reason, you do make him come? Like by some accident? Whatever you do, don't swallow."

I scrunched my nose. "What else am I going to do with it?"

"Act like that shit is acid. Avoid it at all costs. Like you're afraid of it. Say shit like *yuck* and *gross*."

I laughed out loud. "Why?"

"Same reason," she said. "If you swallow, he'll want it all the time. And, that'll be all he wants. He'll just want you to suck his dick. You'll become the blowjob girl. Believe me, you don't want to be that girl. I've been her. It's no fun."

I got a pretty good laugh thinking about it, and then regained my composure. "You've been the blowjob girl?"

She rolled her eyes while she nodded. "Yep. There was this guy. Brad Bishop. I wanted him to give me the dick, and he just wanted to hang out. That's all we did. Hang out. Never even made out. Not once. I was beginning to think he was gay. So, one night, I unzipped his pants and pulled out his dick. 'What are you doing?' That's what he asked me. I didn't even respond, I just wrapped my lips around it. He didn't ask me anything else. He just moaned. Told me it was the best blowjob he ever got."

"And then what happened?"

"Every time I saw him, that was all he wanted. I sucked his dick in the car, in the theater, in his bedroom, in his mom's living room, in the driveway, you name it."

"And he never fucked you?"

She shook her head. "Nope. Because I made the mistake of swallowing *before* we had sex. So what you need to do is this: act like you're afraid of that shit. Then, one day, after he's fucked you for a few weeks or so, tell him you want to try and swallow. Tell him you're willing to give it a go just because you think he's *that cool*. Tell him you like him so much you're going to swallow his cum. He'll never forget it. But only do it after you get the dick."

"So, I should unzip his pants, pull out his dick, and suck it. But don't swallow?"

"Yep."

"And that'll make him like me?"

"It'll make him want you. Then, when he decides to fuck you, fuck him like your life depends on it. Then, he'll like you."

It sounded like pretty good advice. And, according to her, she'd been in her fair share of relationships. Lucky me, because if there was one thing I was good at besides boxing, sucking cocks had to be it.

"Okay. I'll try it. If this makes him hate me, I'm really going to be mad at you."

"You've sucked a dick before, right?" she asked sarcastically.

"Well, I've been thinking about what you said. I think I was the blowjob girl in high school. It seems like that's all I did." I chuckled. "Maybe it was because I always swallowed."

"Probably. You don't ever want to do that until they give you the dick. And then, always make a *huge* deal of it. Like you're taking this big step. It makes them feel special."

"I'll try it," I said. "Thanks."

"Bring him in here."

54

"In *here*?"

"Yeah, I want to see him."

I had no intention of bringing him to the shitty diner I worked at. "I don't think I want to bring him in here. Maybe you can come to the gym sometime. Watch me fight or something."

"Whatever. I just want to see this guy. He sounds hot."

"He is hot. I just hope this works."

"That's what I was going to say a minute ago. Have you ever sucked a guy's dick and had him get mad about it?"

I didn't even have to think about it. "Nope."

"You never will, either. Guys love blowjobs."

I hoped she was right.

And I was ready to find out.

EIGHT

JAZ

Day twenty-six.

"This is awesome, what did you do to it?" Ethan asked.

The chicken tasted much better than the list of ingredients indicated, that was for sure. "Olive oil, fresh basil, salt, and pepper. That's it."

"Really?"

I nodded. "Really."

I had invited Ethan over for dinner and had every intention of following Rachel's recommendation of sucking his cock after we finished our meal. Seeing him satisfied with my cooking was a much better experience than I ever would have expected, and as much as I didn't want it to end, I was ready to move on to stage two of our night.

"Well, it's really good. Like *really* good," he said.

"Thank you."

He was wearing jeans, boots, and a really cute black and white plaid short-sleeved pearl snap shirt. He looked much different than he did in sweats or shorts, which was all I had seen him wear since we'd met. It was obvious his hair had product in it, but it was still kind of everywhere hair, which added to his overall cuteness.

He took another bite. "When's your next fight?"

"Ripp said he's setting up something now. I'd guess here in a few weeks – at the most – from what he said."

"But you don't know who?"

I poked a piece of chicken in my mouth and shrugged. "Don't really care. As long as she's in my weight class, I'm not worried."

"Good attitude to have."

I nodded in agreement. I thought of sucking his cock and wondered if he'd be as pleased with it as he was with the poultry. I took another bite of the mouth-watering chicken and began to wonder.

"Have you dated since..." I paused, not really knowing how to continue. Honestly, I wished I never would have started the question. Luckily, he fully understood what I was too uncomfortable to ask.

"No." The fork dangled from between his thumb and forefinger as he gazed down at the table. "I don't know. I would. But. I just haven't found anyone who interested me enough."

"No sex, either?"

"No. I'm not a random sex kind of guy."

Well, that's good to know.

I wondered if sucking his cock qualified as sex, and if so, if he would consider it random. Maybe he was interested enough in me to let me do it, and all I needed to do was ask.

But Rachel had said not to ask. I was just supposed to do it.

I poked at my chicken, far less interested in eating than I was in luring Ethan into sex. After a lengthy period of silence during which I planned what my next step was going to be, I took another bite and looked at him.

I didn't really have a preference when it came to men, it simply seemed if someone was willing to pay attention to me, I allowed them to. That willingness to attach myself to any man who showered me with attention was a result of my lack of a healthy relationship with my father, and I realized it. My sexual experiences had produced nerds, jocks, cowboys, stoners, and a businessman. They ranged in age from three years younger than me to thirteen years older.

Sitting across the table from Ethan, I was convinced if I was given an opportunity to choose, he would be the type of man I preferred. Breathtakingly handsome, very athletic, and slightly broken, he was the epitome of perfection.

Because he was gorgeous. And imperfect.

Desperately wanting him to finish his chicken so I could suck his cock, I peered across the table. He was one bite away from a blowjob.

Satisfaction washed over me as I watched him spear the last piece of chicken with his fork and raise it to his mouth. I hurriedly finished my meal and stood up, prepared to take our dishes to the kitchen and begin my sexual advance.

I reached for his plate. "Looks like you enjoyed it."

He looked up and grinned. "Is there more?"

Are you fucking kidding me?

"Uhhm. Sure," I responded, even though I wanted to tell him no. "Do you want more?"

"If it's no trouble."

It's not any trouble, but you're cock blocking yourself and you don't even know it.

"No, not at all," I said.

I took his plate to the kitchen and picked through the platter of chicken, looking for the smallest piece. Tempted to cut one of them in half, but afraid he'd raise an eyebrow at the alteration, I reluctantly chose the smallest breast and grabbed the remaining asparagus.

"Here you go," I said, handing him the plate.

"You're not going to eat more?"

My appetite was elsewhere. "I'm stuffed."

I sat down and waited anxiously for him to finish his meal. Not having knowledge of my plans to suck him into a state of sexual bliss, he ate slowly and talked about topics I had very little interest in discussing.

A piece of chicken dangled from the tip of his fork. "So how long have you had your car?"

What in the fuck does that have to do with anything?

I had the car for nothing short of forever. It was the only car I ever owned, and I'd driven it from my sophomore year in high school until its most recent venture to work, one day prior. "Uhhm, for like eight years. I've had it since I was sixteen."

"You just don't see many of those old school Corollas around anymore."

No shit. Most people can afford to replace them.

"Yeah," I said with a roll of my eyes. "It's a classic."

He ate the piece of chicken, took a sip of wine, and inspected the asparagus. After much thought, he stabbed a piece and raised it to his mouth. After nibbling at it leisurely until all that remained was the short stalk that was attached to the tines of his fork, he removed the remaining piece with his fingers.

I wanted to scream.

He looked at it, and upon accepting it as edible, nibbled on it endlessly.

Frustrated beyond belief, I counted the remaining pieces of asparagus.

Six.

I wished I had given him three.

My eyes went to the chicken. It appeared untouched short of the one nibble he had taken.

"Are you full?" I asked, the tone of my voice filled with hope.

"Just taking my time. It's so good. I can't believe you're not going to have any more. You normally eat like a man."

I shrugged. "I'm just full."

Becoming increasingly irritated with each passing second, I ran through the few possibilities I could come up with to ruin his meal.

I could have talked about gross stuff and tried to ruin his appetite, but decided it might curb my sexual desire. My small dining table didn't have a cloth on it, so tugging against the table cloth and causing a spill wasn't an option, and starting a fire was out of the question. While he chewed on another small piece of chicken, I gnawed on my lower lip and continued my line of thought.

Being in his presence as a friend was becoming annoying. It wasn't that I didn't enjoy his company, because I did, but I was far too attracted to him to continue without at least trying to get in his pants.

The wine.

The table was small enough that I just might be able to make it work. I reached for the glass at the exact instant he began to strike up a new conversation.

"So what about you?" he asked. "When was your last relationship?"

I smacked the back of my hand against the glass, toppling it over. The wine spilled with perfection, all over his plate.

And his cute little shirt.

And lap.

Fuck.

I felt like a complete fool.

"Shit!" I shouted.

"Shit," he shouted.

"It was an accident," I said as I jumped from my seat.

He chuckled as he tried to absorb the wine with his napkin. "I didn't think it was intentional."

If you only knew.

I ran to the kitchen, dampened a few towels, and returned to my dining disaster. "Here, I'll get it. I feel like such a klutz."

After cleaning up the mess and taking his plate to the kitchen, I took a close look at his shirt. It had a six-inch wide swath of wine down the center of the bottom half of it.

My accelerated blowjob plan had gone to fuck, and I felt like an absolute fool. I motioned toward the rapidly drying stain on his shirt. "You should probably take it off so I can wash it."

Without hesitation, he tugged against each side of the shirt, popping the snaps from the bottom to the top. With a quick shrug of his shoulders he dropped the shirt down his arms and handed it to me.

Now standing in front of me wearing only his jeans and boots, I realized several things. One, it was the first time I had seen him shirtless. Two, I was halfway to having him completely naked. And, three, there was no way he was getting out of my home without me at least sucking his cock.

His wide chest tapered down to a perfectly chiseled mid-section. Where most men hoped to have a six-pack, he had an eight-pack. How lower stomach formed into the shape of a 'V', which pointed directly to the prize housed in the jeans that hung low on his waist.

Every time I had seen him in the gym, he was dressed in shorts or sweats, but he always wore a tee shirt or hoodie. I tore my eyes from his massive chest and swollen biceps. "At least it was a Chardonnay."

He seemed slightly self-conscious.

"I'd give you a shirt, but there's no way--"

"I'm okay with it if you are," he interrupted.

Now that he had his shirt off, I never wanted to see him with it on again.

I raised his wadded shirt, shrugged, and turned away. "Considering the circumstances..."

Three steps toward the laundry room I had a revelation. I turned around. "You didn't get anything on your jeans did you?"

He looked down. I looked down. I had a reason to stare, and I used it. A dark spot on the hip of the jeans gave me a little hope. I stepped closer. Sure enough, a spot the size of my fist darkened the hip of his jeans.

My bumbling the glass of wine was a complete success!

I pointed to the spot. The longer I looked at it, the less it looked like a wine stain. I declared the spot a product of my disaster nonetheless. "There's a spot right there."

"I can wash them when I get home," he said.

You're taking those jeans off, mister.

I shrugged. "I guess you can, but it'll stain for sure. I think you've only got like thirty minutes, and then Chardonnay stains for good."

His eyes went wide. "Really?"

Fuck I don't know, but it sounds good.

"It's a well-known wine fact. Just uhhm. I'll grab you some shorts. I've got a few large pair of swishy shorts I wear around the house. You can wear one of them until they're clean."

"Okay," he said.

I did a mental fist pump and ran to my room. A moment later I had returned with the shorts.

I handed them to him. "Here."

"Where do you want me to change?"

You can take them off right there.

"In the bathroom?"

"Okay."

He came out of the bathroom in a matter of seconds, the shorts clinging to his muscular thighs and shapely ass like a thick layer of shiny blue paint. In the front, a prominent bulge reminded me of why I'd spilled the wine in the first place.

I guess they're not big enough. Oh darn.

"They're kind of…" He tugged down on the front of the shorts. "Small."

"They're as big as I've got." They weren't, but it sounded good.

I walked in his direction, my eyes shifting between his abs and his bulge as I approached. I held my hand out. "It should just be an hour or so to wash and dry them."

An hour with him wearing my tiny silk shorts was going to be nothing short of heaven. I carried the clothes to the laundry, sprayed them with stain remover, and placed them in the wash. I rushed back into the living room, eager to see my tiny shorts wearing soon-to-be sexual partner.

Sitting on the loveseat with his legs crossed, he looked like he belonged in a *Saturday Night Live* skit. I fought against the urge to laugh and sat down at his side. "Sorry I ruined your dinner."

He smiled a little, but it wasn't very convincing. "I was getting full anyway."

I studied his long muscular legs and quickly realized they were hairless. Surprised that I had never noticed before, but intrigued that he appeared to shave his legs, I stared for a moment just to be sure.

Yep. Sans hair.

"Do you shave your legs?"

"Yeah. I really don't like hair – other than on my head. Does it bother you?"

It did everything *but* bother me. It explained his hairless torso. I gazed at his legs. I wanted to caress them, squeezing his bulging thigh muscles in my dainty little hands as I worked my way up to his stiff cock.

"No. Uhhm. Not at all. I uhhm. I think it's sexy."

"Really?"

My eyes moved to his shorts.

Shit!

The surprise blowjob wasn't going to be so easy after all. With him wearing the skin-tight shorts, my plan of unzipping his pants and easily removing his cock was thwarted. Now, the only way to get to his cock was to get him to remove the shorts – and there was no doubt in my mind that getting him to take them off would require lengthy negotiations.

That wasn't part of the plan.

I decided to take a chance. I reached for his leg and rested my hand on the smooth skin of his tanned thigh. Much to my surprise, he didn't object. My heartbeat increased tenfold. My face went hot. I slid my hand a little further. My heart rose into my throat.

I sighed. "Yeah, really."

The rush of sexual emotions made me feel like I was a horny

adolescent again, and I liked it.

A lot.

I slid my hand closer to the prize.

Silence.

Maybe Rachel was right. Maybe all guys loved blowjobs just like she said, and Ethan would stand as no exception. Maybe if I could figure out a way to fit my fingers between the fabric of the shorts and his muscular thigh, I could just reach up there and get started by stroking it.

Maybe if I took it a few inches of thigh at a time he wouldn't even notice. At least not until it was too late.

I stared at the wall in front of me and slid my hand up his thigh a few more inches. Then, a few more. I didn't dare look in his direction, fear of rejection prevented it. He had to realize I was working my way up his thigh, and so far, he hadn't complained. Convinced he was satisfied with my plan to fondle his cock, I blindly slid my hand further. And then, the unmistakably smooth skin of a cock's head was against my hand.

What the fuck?

I glanced at his lap. Half of his hard cock stuck out the bottom of the leg opening of his tiny shorts.

And my hand was on it.

I quickly made eye contact.

He grinned.

There was no turning back.

"Take them off?" The words escaped my lips in the form of a dry whisper.

Apparently, it was enough for him to understand my desire.

He stood up, and after a slight struggle, pushed the shorts past his cock and down his legs. During the grueling process of him removing his undersized shorts, I took all of his completely naked body into view. Every inch of him was hairless, tan, smooth, and...

Oversized.

I realized I had many options as far as positioning myself to suck his cock. Instead of complicating matters, I settled into the couch cushion, extended my arm, and curled my index finger into my palm repeatedly.

Come here, you big sexy fucker.

Unwilling to wait any longer than I had to, I scooted to the outermost edge of the couch and wet my lips with my tongue. He and his throbbing third leg stepped in front of me, and without his expressed permission or taking time to explain my desires, I grabbed his cock and began sucking my way into his heart.

In the desolate area where I grew up, most girls had some form of talent. Some were good at cooking. Others grew up on farms and were quite talented at riding horses or driving tractors. As fate would have it, my talents were limited to boxing, sucking cocks, and fucking.

And I was good all of them.

I flattened the back of my tongue and forced as much of his swollen shaft into my throat as I could. It wasn't easy, but the look on Ethan's face made it rewarding. If I learned nothing more from all of my sexual experiences, I learned to watch the expression on the man's face who I was attempting to please.

And Ethan was pleased.

I knew if he was pleased with what I had done so far, he'd really be pleased once I got my rhythm.

With him standing directly in front of the couch and me sitting at the edge of the cushion, I gripped his muscular ass in my hands and began to suck his cock like it was going to solve all the world's problems.

I massaged his balls carefully in my hand while I slid my mouth up and down the thick shaft with precision. The fleshy tip banged deep into my throat with each stroke of my lips. Satisfied that I was well on my way to etching a permanent mark deep in Ethan's mind, I continued to suck vigorously, hoping my talent would satisfy him so greatly that he made me a permanent part of his leisurely evening schedule.

Measuring my success in boxing came easy. I simply compared the wins to the losses. As there weren't any losses, I was easily able to identify myself as a success.

Determining my success at sucking a man's dick was equally as easy. It wasn't indicated by moans, groans, or an appreciative post-blowjob comment. At least in my mind, it was measured in the amount of time it took me to get a man to reach climax. If I was somehow able to coerce a man to reach orgasm – simply by using my mouth – in a matter of a few minutes, he was undoubtedly satisfied with my performance.

If I had to suck and stroke endlessly until my jaw, hands, arms, and mouth were exhausted, something was either wrong with me – or him. Based on the available information and my willingness to fully accept it, I didn't require praise in boxing or in my head game. Everything I needed was in front of me.

I massaged his smooth ball sack and moved my wet mouth along the shaft, studying his facial expression as I did so.

I buried him deep into my throat and gazed up and into his eyes.

He lifted his chin and tilted his head back. His entire body tensed and he began to moan. I recalled what Rachel said about not sucking him to completion, but at that moment, while caught up in the excitement of it all, I wasn't about to stop.

I was ninety seconds into my performance and he was going to unleash.

I wanted to see it.

I *needed* to see it.

Something about watching a man ejaculate was exciting to me. Seeing the cum spurt from the tip of his cock made me feel like I had truly accomplished something.

And it was fucking hot.

As his cock twitched and began to swell, his moaning deepened, and I slid his cock from my throat in response.

Holding it directly in front of my mouth, I jacked my hands along the slippery shaft, pointing the tip into my waiting and willing mouth.

In two more strokes, I was well on my way to success. His chest tensed, his bicep muscles flared, and he groaned out in pleasure. Cum blasted from the tip of his cock and shot into my mouth over and over, the long thick bursts seeming to last forever.

I'd sucked enough cocks in my younger years to develop a taste for a man's cum. It wasn't something I would describe as *tasty*, but it was somehow satisfying in its own way. I found the salty and slightly bitter essence to be rather sensual. A reminder of the sensuous act that extracted it from deep within.

As his cum filled my mouth, however, my tongue tried to reject it. My stomach heaved. My nostrils flared.

And I remembered.

Asparagus.

Fuck.

Nothing on this earth made a person's piss stink – or a man's cum taste – worse than asparagus.

He gazed into my eyes.

I met his gaze. With my mouth agape, his cock still in my hand, and my tongue covered in his rotten cum, I tried my hardest to look content.

I fought against the putrid stench, closed my mouth, and swallowed.

My stomach fought to reject it.

I struggled to keep it down.

And I remembered Rachel's advice.

Whatever you do, don't swallow.

Truer words had never been spoken.

NINE

JAZ

Day twenty-nine.

It had been three days since the blowjob incident, and it appeared sucking Ethan's cock was the best decision I could have ever made. We now communicated several times daily, and he seemed to be far more interested in me sexually and personally.

While in my cooldown mode of my training, I was explaining my next scheduled fight.

"Next week?" he asked. "Really?"

"He said she was like begging for a chance. After she heard what I did to that Linda Lopez chick, she's been trying to get at me. Ripp didn't even have to ask. Her trainer or manager or whatever called him."

"You don't think it's too soon?"

"Too soon?" I smacked the speedbag again. "No."

"I just…"

I smacked the bag again. "You just what?"

"I don't want you to get hurt."

I hit it again and turned toward him. The bag bounced back and forth on the rebound platform. "Hurt?" I coughed out a laugh. "Don't worry about that. I won't get hurt."

"You can never be sure. If it's too soon, would you tell him?"

I rolled my eyes. "Sure. But it's not. I don't know what that even means. I went one round with that chick, and it's been almost a week. If I had ten back-to-back fights like that it'd be equal to only one *real* fight."

"It's just. I don't know." He dropped his gaze to my feet, held it for a second, and then lifted his eyes to meet mine. "I care about you, and I don't want anything to happen."

Awwe.

Apparently the blowjob thing worked.

"Thank you. But it'll be fine."

He twisted his mouth to the side and shrugged.

I hit the bag again, once with each hand, then sighed. "No girl is going to hurt me. She might beat me but she won't hurt me."

"I don't know how you can say that."

I looked at his gloved hands. I glanced around the gym. It was early evening, and several of the rings were empty, including the one closest to us.

I motioned toward the ring. "Come on."

"What?"

"Get in the ring."

"No. I can't get in there with you."

"Why not?"

"I don't want to…"

"What? Hurt me? That's my point. You won't. Come on."

"Jaz, seriously."

I walked to the ring, ducked under the ropes, and climbed inside. He remained standing beside the speed bag.

"Pussy," I taunted.

He puffed his chest. "Excuse me?"

"You said the other day that you'd like fighting with me."

He glanced over each shoulder. "Yeah, maybe at home."

"Scared of what people are going to say?"

"No."

I tapped my gloves together. "Come on, pussy."

The thought of Ethan getting in the ring with me made my pussy throb. I hadn't shared my sexual preferences with him yet, but I was pretty sure when I did, he'd be shocked. I liked my sex no differently than my fights.

Fast and rough.

He glanced over each of his shoulders again.

"Quit worrying about who's going to see you or what someone's going to think," I complained.

He appeared to be considering it.

"There's only one way to live life. Like nobody's watching."

He turned toward me, walked to the base of the ring, and climbed inside. I held my gloves at arm's length.

He pounded his gloves against mine.

I poked a quick jab at him. As he took a step back, I swung an uppercut toward his jaw.

Wham!

The tip of my glove connected hard with his chin. He stumbled, clearly shocked at the speed – and the force – of my punch.

He shook his head. "You don't hit like a…"

A left hook to his ribs made him cough out his remaining breath and prevented him from finishing his sentence.

I wasn't about to give him any mercy, especially when he was worried about me getting hurt. I needed to prove a point, and I was well on my way to doing so. I threw a combination of punches into his mid-section, and he naturally reacted by swinging an uppercut toward my chin.

The punch wasn't weak, and it sure wasn't intended for a girl. He swung it naturally, out of a fighter's desire to survive in the ring. If it would have connected, it probably would have knocked me out.

I leaned back, and his glove swung past me, narrowly missing my jaw. A right cross counter on my part connected well with his shoulder, knocking him slightly off-balance. After securing my footing, I swung a left hook into the back of his right shoulder, spinning him around slightly.

Another quick hook to his kidney almost dropped him to his knees.

"I don't hit like what? Like a girl?"

He stumbled to regain his footing, and while he did, I stepped back and admired him.

I'd always wanted to fight with my respective other, but had yet to date – or even fuck – a boxer or fighter. Until Ethan, I had never been in the ring with one of my sexual interests.

I now realized that my original suspicions were correct. I liked it. And I liked it a lot. Fighting with him was a huge turn-on, and my wet pussy was proof.

"No," he said. He turned around quickly, bringing a wild left with him.

The punch caught me on the right side of the jaw, blurring my vision and making me see stars. Naturally, I took a few steps backward and raised my forearms to protect my face.

It was the first time I had been hit in almost ten years, and the very first time anyone had made me see stars.

My pussy was soaked.

I lowered my gloves, stepped toward him, and extended my arms.

He tapped his gloves against mine. "You alright?"

"Are you kidding? Never been better," I said. I lowered the tone of my voice to a whisper. "My pussy is soaked."

"Seriously?" he asked.

I nodded. "Completely. Soaked."

"That's weird. I doubt being hit hard would make my cock stiff," he said.

He barely completed the sentence. When he said the word *my*, I swung a right uppercut. Just as he finished the speaking, the punch caught the underside of his chin, knocking him senseless for an instant.

As he stumbled, I stepped back and admired my work. "You should know for sure now," I said with a laugh. "Is it hard?"

"What on God's green little earth is going on here?"

I turned toward the voice.

Fuck. Kelsey.

He stood beside the ring with his hands on his hips and his face clearly expressing the disgust he felt. He met my gaze, held it for a second, and then turned toward Ethan. After a short glare, he looked at me again.

"Was your name Jaz or Spaz?" he asked. "I can't remember."

I swallowed and cleared my throat. "Jaz."

"Huh," he said. "I would have guessed the other."

He shook his head and walked away.

"Is he pissed?" I whispered.

Ethan nodded. "He sure looked like it."

"Had enough?" I asked, my voice filled with sarcasm.

He coughed out a laugh and nodded. "You proved your point."

"What makes you think I was trying to prove a point?" I asked.

He ducked under the ropes, and turned to face me before climbing out. "My sore jaw."

His jaw was sore and my pussy was soaked. "Be sure and put your gloves in your bag," I said. "Don't leave 'em in your locker."

"Why's that?"

"Because," I said. "I need to release some tension before the fight. I was thinking we'd do this at my apartment, later."

He narrowed his eyes and stared.

I climbed from the ring and grinned. "Naked."

The look on his face was all the response I needed.

TEN

JAZ

Day twenty-nine.

Ethan stood in the middle of my living room, wearing nothing but his boxing gloves. His cock hung heavily between his legs, not completely hard, but not soft by any stretch of the imagination. "How hard?" he asked.

I glanced down at his cock and then lifted my eyes to meet his. God, he was so fucking sexy. "Hard enough I remember it," I responded.

I lowered my hands.

He punched me in the center of the face, knocking me off-balance and almost toppling me over. Tears ran down my cheeks. Not tears from crying, but tears caused by being hit right in the middle of my nose.

I shook my head and wished I could wipe my watering eyes, but the boxing gloves I was wearing prevented it.

"Enough?" he asked.

It wasn't. I didn't feel the rush of sexual emotion yet. Not like I did when Kelsey caught us in the ring. Maybe I needed to hit him. "Tighten your jaw muscles."

He narrowed his eyes and lowered his hands.

"You sure you're ready?"

He blinked and nodded slightly.

I swung a hard right cross, landing right on the tip of his chin. He stumbled three or four steps to the rear, eventually catching his balance and shaking his head from side to side. "Holy shit," he exclaimed. "You hit hard as fuck."

"Good to know," I said. "I've always wondered."

I stole a glance at his cock. It was slightly harder than before. My pussy began to tingle at the thought of fighting and fucking at the same time. I pounded my gloves against my stomach. "Give me a good three or four to the body."

I was wearing a plaid skirt, no panties, and a sports bra. Considering the size of my boobs, the sports bra was mandatory. The plaid skirt, however, was optional. A request on Ethan's part to fulfill some ridiculous fantasy.

A commando schoolgirl boxer.

"Are you sure?"

"Hurry up," I demanded. "I'm getting horny as fuck."

I extended my arms to the side, giving him a free shot at my torso. He unleashed a three-punch combo to my mid-section, pulling his punches slightly. The quick series of half-power blows knocked me back about six feet and caused the breath to shoot from my lungs.

As I fought to breathe there was no doubt in my mind that my pussy was soaked. "Put 'em up," I howled.

His eyes widened. He raised his gloves. I stepped toward him and as soon as I was within reach, we exchanged blows for several long seconds, me hitting him with all I had, and him returning punches that were packed with about half the power he was capable of unleashing.

Thirty seconds later, and I was covered from head to toe in sweat, and my arms felt like Jell-O. I was done with the fighting, and was ready to move on to the fucking.

I lowered my tired self to my knees. "Stick…your cock…in my…mouth," I said between breaths.

He didn't hesitate. In three short steps, his hips were against my face and his rather flaccid cock was in my mouth. I realized, just like Rachel predicted I would be, that I was the blowjob girl. But. I was preparing to become the boxer in the plaid skirt who fucked Ethan senseless.

I wrapped my arms around his waist and pulled against his ass with my gloves, more for my benefit than his. Something about having a man's ass in my hands while I sucked his cock made me wetter than wet. I sucked on his rapidly growing shaft until it filled my throat. Four or five good gagging fits later, and I stood up with watering eyes.

He returned a worried stare.

"Don't worry," I said with a grin. "I'm gonna give you the good stuff."

I turned toward the couch and bent over. With my boobs buried in the cushion and my ass high in the air, I reached for my skirt, only to quickly remember I was wearing boxing gloves. Half a dozen unsuccessful attempts to raise my skirt over my ass later, and I surrendered the idea and glanced over my shoulder.

Completely naked with the exception of his red and white boxing gloves, Ethan stood behind me wide-eyed and rock hard.

"Just fuck me," I demanded.

He pounded his gloves together as if preparing to begin a fight.

He lifted his bare foot and easily flipped the back of my skirt over my ass and onto the back side of my hips. His gloves squeezed my waist. With neither of us able to guide his throbbing cock into my wet and willing hole, it danced around between my legs for some time before finally landing perfectly centered between my pussy lips.

Before we got started, I needed to make sure we were on the same page, sexually speaking. "I want it rough."

His cock still hovered in mid-air, tickling my pussy with each breath he took. He cleared his throat. "Rough?"

"Rough as fuck," I assured him.

With one hard shove, he filled me with cock and forced the air from my lungs.

I grunted like I'd been gut-punched.

Holy fuck. That's a lot of cock.

"Are you alright?"

I raised my right glove high in the air and waved it. "I'm good," I lied.

I felt like I was being fucked by an arm. I knew his cock was big, but I didn't realize just how large it actually was. With it shoved balls-deep inside of me, I was quickly reminded that it had been a long time since I'd had sex. Furthermore, I had a newfound awareness that my ability to comparatively measure a cock based on memory alone wasn't a strength I possessed.

I bit into my bottom lip and mentally prepared for the sexual beating I'd been hoping for.

Ethan didn't disappoint.

I felt like I was losing my virginity – again – and I loved it.

Blazing a brand new path down a previously traveled road, he thrust his way deep into my memory bank. Leaving a permanent mental impression with each savage thrust, he pounded every inch of himself into me without reservation.

Jesus. Fucking. Christ.

We were just getting started, and absolutely nothing or no one prior to him mattered. Ethan had bought and paid for my pussy in the first few strokes, and with each additional thrust he was paying his rent well into the future.

Two minutes into our sexual adventure, and he owned me.

Owned. Me.

His cock now fit me like a glove. His hips slapped against my ass with precision. I no longer felt like I was being ripped apart. I was only being fucked. And fucked good. It was the kind of sex that a girl thinks about for a lifetime. The one sexual adventure that all future sex would be compared to.

Each stroke brought an entire mind full of sexual emotion, and it all seemed new to me. While I attempted to process just what it was I was feeling, he would withdraw himself, taking away all of the feelings I was trying desperately to identify. Immediately, he would shove me full once more, bringing another dose of sensual overload.

He pounded himself into me deeply. The small living room smelled like sweat, sex, and testosterone.

Whatever had happened to me in the past wasn't sex. This? This was sex. This was what songs were written about, movies were produced in an effort to replicate, and books were written about in an attempt to explain.

"Hit me," I bellowed.

"What?"

"Hit me."

I wanted to talk dirty to him, explaining what I felt and what I wanted, but I couldn't. He had fucked me into a reduced state of mental being, and I was no longer capable of reasoning. It wasn't that I didn't want to be vocal during our sexual encounter, I was simply incapable of using my mind for much more than my feeble attempts to identify what I was feeling.

"Where?" he asked.

It took me a minute to realize just what he was asking me. Only after clearing my mind of the blissful thoughts that filled it did I remember that I'd all but demanded that he hit me.

"Anywhere," I responded.

He playfully tapped the side of my head with the inside of his right glove. The smell of leather filled my nostrils. It reminded me of the gym, fighting, and our little living room brawl. It was exactly what I had hoped for, but I wanted more.

"Harder. Ass. Face. I don't care," I growled. "Just hit me. Hit me and fuck me."

He continued to fuck me rhythmically, his hands lightly bouncing off the sides of my face and the back of my ass while he did so.

I was about to reach climax.

"Harder," I grunted.

His gloves began to rain down on me, one after the other, while he continued to fuck me. His balls banged against my pussy. His hands banged against the side of my face. And, his cock banged against spots inside of me I was unaware even existed.

My mind escaped me and my legs began to shake.

I arched my back and cried out. "Holy fuuuuuck!"

I felt his cock swell, and he did the same.

"Aaaarrrghhh," he growled.

The orgasm worked its way from my toes to my temples. Simultaneously, a tingling from deep inside my pussy seemed to burst well within me, leaving me in an almost confused state of being. I buried my face into the couch cushion and screamed. It was an orgasm unlike anything I had felt in the past, and I was certain – at least at that moment – that I would never live to feel another like it again.

A few seconds into my sexual release, and I realized he wasn't done fucking me. Still groaning into the now silent room, his cock burst inside of me, causing me to reach climax again, in a different fashion altogether.

He held his cock in place and continued to groan. My body shook and shuddered, exhausted from the fighting, the sex, and the two-hour workout that led to it all.

My upper body collapsed onto the couch. He flopped down beside me. I felt his cum run down my inner thigh.

I didn't care.

We turned our heads to face one another.

"That was fucking hot," he said.

"Uh huh," I murmured. "Your cock. It's--"

"Too big?"

I was going to say huge.

"No," I said. "It's perfect."

"Good, because there for a while I was afraid it wasn't going to fit in your tight little pussy."

You're not the only one.

"You like it?"

He blinked his eyes and sighed. "Yeah."

"Good," I said. "Because now it's ruined."

He blinked and stared. "What do you mean?"

Believe me, you'd never understand.

83

"Nothing," I lied. "I think I'm delirious."
And that, at least, was true.

ELEVEN

JAZ

Day thirty-three.

"Oh my God, already?" she asked.

I finished wiping off the table and sat down. "What do you mean *already*?" I moved the condiment caddy back to the center of the table and waited for her to respond.

"Well," she said. "You just sucked his cock the other night."

"And on the first night that we talked about him you accused me of acting like I was fifteen. And you told me not to be the blowjob girl. How long do most *adults* wait to fuck?"

She shrugged. "I just go for it."

"Yeah," I said with a sarcastic grin. "Me too."

She placed her hands on her hips and shot me a look. "So?"

I wanted to tell her all the sordid details, but decided to make her beg for them. "What?"

"Does he have a nice dick?"

Yeah, if he was a fucking horse.

I shrugged. "Yeah."

"Was he any good?"

Any good? He fucked me into a state of mental retardation.

"Yeah."

85

"Yeah, huh? Just yeah?"

I felt giddy about it all, and I couldn't wait to tell someone, and she was the only *someone* I had. "His body is solid muscle, his cock is the size of my arm, and he's got the stamina of a true porn star. He fucked me until I couldn't talk, think, or even fucking see straight. And that's the truth."

She stood with her mouth agape and stared. "Really?"

I nodded. "Uh huh."

"You got any pics of his dick?"

"Seriously? No. I was too busy moaning and having orgasms to take any pics."

"He hasn't sent you one single pic of his dick?"

"Sent me one?"

"Yeah. Sent you one."

"No," I said. It seemed like a ridiculous question on her part, so I had to ask. "Do guys actually do that?"

She looked at me with crazy eyes. "Really?"

I shrugged. "Yeah."

"They do it all the time. You know, to try and get you interested."

And therein lied the only explanation I needed. The fact it never happened to me made perfect sense. I typically gave up the pussy pretty quickly, hence the lack of need for guys to coerce me with pics of their dicks.

"Huh," I said. "Maybe they do it here, but not in Nebraska. Not where I'm from."

"Oh, I forgot you were from the sticks."

I chuckled. "No dick pics in the sticks."

"So he's got a big dick, huh?"

I inhaled a deep breath and let half of it out, responding as I exhaled. "Massive."

She sat down, tossed her towel on the table in front of her, and cleared her throat. "I had this guy I was fucking when I was in high school. His name was Steve. Steve Cooley. His dick was huge. I was a senior and he was like, I don't know, maybe twenty-two years old. My parents acted like he was forty. Anyway. So we were out on a date and I thought I needed to suck his dick to keep him interested, so I offered. And he whipped it out. I just stared. I'd only seen a few dicks at the time, and they were both high school dicks, so my dumb ass was convinced all older guys had great big dicks. Like they grew a few more inches when they got out of school."

I laughed. "They don't?"

"I don't think so. They don't grow like that. Do they?"

I was joking, initially. Now she had me wondering. I spoke my way through my thought process. "Well, at some point they do, or babies would have great big dicks. I used to baby sit, and I can assure you babies don't have 'em. So, maybe it's like arms and legs, and cocks quit growing when the other stuff quits."

"So, when a guy reaches full height, and he's not growing any more, his dick is at full size?"

"I suppose so," I said.

"Well, my younger brother kept getting taller until he was like twenty-one. His junior year in college, he finally stopped. Six foot four. So, is it just a height thing?"

I shrugged.

"When guys get thicker, when they fill out, do their cocks get thicker?" she asked.

It was a good question. Ethan was lean and muscular, and his cock was as fat as my wrist. I couldn't imagine it getting any thicker. Hopefully he wouldn't ever gain weight, and I wouldn't have to worry about it.

"You know," she said. "When guys gain weight, they get thick all over. Arms, legs, waist, neck. All of it. You know?"

She had a great point. I tried to imagine Ethan slightly overweight, and grew sick at the thought of it.

"So this Steve guy. Did you ever fuck him?" I asked.

"Oh, hell yes. We fucked like rabbits. Until my dad found out."

"Was he the biggest you've ever had?"

"Yeah. Biggest ever."

"Was it different? You know, was there a difference between his and everyone else's? I mean, I know there was in size, but was there a difference in what it felt like?"

Before she answered, I felt a need to correct myself. "Did it make you *feel* different? You know, was the sex different?"

She gazed beyond me, inhaled a deep breath, and exhaled without ever focusing on me. "Best sex ever."

"Were the orgasms different than with the other guys?"

"Oh, hell yes. Orgasms with him? I can still remember 'em. Once, I had one so hard that I couldn't get my legs to work. I couldn't fucking walk. I'm serious. I had to sleep it off. I couldn't even get up to go to the bathroom."

"No shit?"

"Yeah. The orgasms I had with him made my legs shake, and they made me act dumb sometimes. You've heard people say 'fuck your brains out?' Well, that's true. Kind of. He'd fuck me and there were times

I'd look around his room like I'd never seen it before. Like everything was new. Then, ten minutes later, I'd be okay. Oh, and before him? One orgasm, and that was it. When *he* fucked me? I'd have six or seven. It was crazy."

"So what happened with your dad?"

"Oh. Yeah. It was a bad deal. I'd missed my period, and I thought I was pregnant. I was scared, and I told my mom. So, we went and got a test, and I wasn't. But what did she do? Told my dad. And then he went to Steve's house and threatened him. I got grounded. After that, it was all over. He moved away right after that."

"You got grounded for thinking you were pregnant?"

She shook her head and laughed. "No. I got grounded for dating a guy my dad prohibited me from dating."

Most parental decisions fascinated me. My father never gave two shits what I did or who I saw, he hated me regardless. A parent attempting to protect their child from harm didn't seem like a bad thing at all. I acted shocked for the sheer sake of conversation. "He forbid you?"

"Yeah. He did shit like that all the time. House parties? God. Every weekend he'd threaten me."

"Did you go?"

"Yeah. Didn't you?"

I pretty much did whatever I wanted without fear of *additional* repercussion. "Sure."

"Back to the big cock thing," I said. "So since then, have you had the six or seven orgasm thing again?"

She shook her head. "Not yet."

"No big cocks since?"

"Not like Steve's," she said with a laugh. "Probably never will be."

89

"That sucks."

"Tell me about it."

"Do you miss it?" I asked.

"Only every time I have sex."

I wondered what my sex life would be like if Ethan never fucked me again. I sat silently and stared out into the parking lot, questioning if it would be better to stop, or truly have him ruin me forever by fucking me for a few weeks or a month and then deciding he wanted to stop.

"So do you think Steve's cock ruined you?"

"What do you mean?"

I hated to rub salt into an open wound, so to speak, but I really wanted to know. "Did it make it hard for you to be truly satisfied with whoever you're fucking now?"

Her eyes dropped to the floor and she shrugged. After a moment's thought, she looked up. "Kind of. It's just, now? Now I always think about what it would be like if the guy I'm fucking had Steve's dick."

And that was what I was afraid of.

It may have been premature by some people's standards, but it was time Ethan and I had a talk.

About his cock.

TWELVE

JAZ

Day thirty-six.

"Actually, Ripp hates the stuff. He only came here because he was helping me out that day, and I wanted to ride in his car," Ethan said.

"So it was just a fluke that you guys caught me here?"

"Pretty much."

"Well, I'm glad you did."

"So am I."

I took a drink of my coffee and considered whether or not the coffee shop was a good place to talk about my dilemma. I looked around the seating area and decided it was as private as my living room, as long as no one showed up.

We were sharing a corner of a small outdoor table, seated only a few feet from one another. Ethan relaxed in his chair, rocking it back onto the rear legs. He seemed more comfortable than he did when we first met, and although he still didn't talk a lot, he did communicate more than he did at first.

As always, his hair was a perfect mess. His clothes – jeans, a tee shirt, and boots – were a reminder that we weren't on a post-workout coffee run, and that our encounter was more of a scheduled event. I liked seeing him dressed the way he was, but doing so made me want him sexually.

Hell, everything made me want him sexually.

Regardless of what he wore, it was difficult to look at Ethan and not want to fuck him. I felt slight guilt for always thinking about having sex with him, but the guilt didn't last long.

"Can I ask you some questions?"

He lowered the chair onto its front legs and removed his sunglasses. "Sure."

"Some serious ones?"

"Am I in trouble?" he asked.

I stared back at him and smiled. I loved his eyes. Absolutely loved them. "No."

"Go for it."

My serious conversations involving men were limited to Freddy, my father, and a few of the guys I had dated over the years. Short of Freddy, none of the men placed any merit on my opinions, though. I wasn't convinced all men were self-righteous pricks, but I did have my suspicions.

I had decided I would tell Ethan what my concerns were, see what he thought, and make my decision on how to proceed with matters based on his responses. I didn't expect him to commit to me, nor was a sure I wanted to commit to him, at least not yet.

As ridiculous as it sounded, I wanted confirmation that he intended to continue fucking me. I didn't care what we chose to call our situation, I was concerned with more important things.

The most important thing.

Cock.

"How long have we known each other?" I asked.

"A month. Give or take."

"Things have changed between us here lately, and I want to discuss it."

He looked worried. "Okay."

"We're fucking now."

He returned an awkward stare. "Is that bad?"

"No," I said. "It's not bad, it's just. I don't want it to stop."

"Okay."

Ethan wasn't opposing me, but he sure wasn't making me feel comfortable that he was vested in our conversation, either.

"I've got this fear that you're going to walk away, and I'm going to be…"

It seemed strange telling him I was concerned that his big cock was going to ruin me from being able to be satisfied in the future. The longer I struggled with choosing the words to finish my sentence, the more ridiculous the entire conversation seemed.

I was mid-sentence into my explanation, and I wished I hadn't even started our little cock talk.

"I'm not going anywhere."

I appreciated the reassurance, but I wasn't convinced. "Give me a second. I wasn't done with my thought, and I need to think of how to say it."

"Okay."

My brain was mush. I'd never been one for beating around the bush, and there was no sense in starting now.

"You've got a really nice cock," I said.

He seemed embarrassed, but eventually he smiled. "Thanks."

"*Really* nice. And. Well. I was afraid that in a few weeks I'd be

93

ruined, and then…you know…it'd be impossible to be satisfied in the future."

There. I said it.

He stared back at me as if waiting for me to continue. I returned his stare, waiting for his response.

His brow wrinkled and his eyes narrowed. "I'm lost. You said a minute ago that you didn't want to stop doing it. Then, you said if we continued, you'd be ruined. Did I hurt you or something?"

"Hurt me?"

"Yeah." He gestured toward my crotch. "Tear your junk up?"

My junk?

"No." I chuckled. "You didn't tear me up."

He looked confused. "So what are we talking about?"

"I said I wanted some commitment from you that you weren't going to just…I don't know…walk away. You know, that you weren't planning on hittin' it and quitin' it. Not that that's never happened, because it has. But if it happens with you, I'd rather it happen now than after a while. I just don't want to be left, you know, struggling to have orgasms later in life because I'm all hung up on thick cocks and I can't find one after you're gone. I know there aren't any assurances in a deal like this, but I was wanting…I was hoping that you'd tell me that you weren't planning on…" I cleared my throat. "Are you going to fuck me again?"

His eyes went wide. "Wow."

I scrunched my nose and glared. "What?"

"You *are* a girl."

"What do you mean?"

"You fight like a man. You walk like a man. You talk like a man. Well, when you cuss, anyway. But *that*? Whatever that was? That was

94

one hundred percent girl. It made no sense whatsoever."

"Which part?"

"All of it."

I had explained everything. For as polite and as attentive as he was, he was a complete man.

Never paying attention to what a woman says.

"I'll dumb it down for you."

"Dumb it down?"

I nodded. "Uh huh."

"When do you plan on walking away?" I asked.

His forehead wrinkled. "From what?"

I sighed. "This."

The confused look returned. "This?"

I inhaled a deep breath and shook my head. "When are you going to quit fucking me?"

"I've got to quit?"

I couldn't help but laugh. "No. But sooner or later, you will. Nothing lasts forever. So, what's your plan?"

He shrugged. "Are you afraid of commitment or something?"

Commitment?

"Commitment?"

"Yeah," he said. "Commitment."

Somehow the conversation had gone from fucking to commitment. As much as I enjoyed their company, men seemed to simply drive me insane. "No, I'm not afraid of commitment. Why?"

"I really don't know what it is you're trying to do here, but maybe this will help." He leaned forward and placed his hand on my knee. "I'm not going to *hit it and quit it*. I like you. If I didn't, I would have never come over for dinner. You didn't ask, but I'm sure you wonder, so I'll just tell you now. I'm not fucking anyone else, and I won't. I'm not like that."

As he spoke, my mouth curled into what eventually became a monstrous grin.

"And, I'm not planning on leaving you," he continued. "I might have been raised by an asshole, but I was raised with a pretty good understanding of what's right and wrong. So when I agreed to have sex, I made a mental commitment to you. You can call it whatever you want to call it."

He lifted his hand from my knee and relaxed in his chair. "I call it being a man."

His little speech almost brought me to tears. I fought to swallow, but my throat had gone dry. I took a drink of coffee and smiled.

"I don't have any more questions."

THIRTEEN

JAZ

Day forty-three.

I ran through the house, tearing clothes off and tossing them aside as I rushed to get to the shower.

I had picked up an extra shift at work to help with the cost of gas from driving back and forth to the gym, and now I was running later than I expected. If I was late for the fight, it would be forfeited, and Ripp would kill me.

I took a quick shower, dried off, and began to rub my lotion on.

The doorbell rang.

Fuck.

I pulled on some sweats and a hoodie, then ran to the window. Peering through the blinds and out onto the entrance revealed no one.

Fucking kids.

I hurried back to my bedroom, got undressed, and quickly put on my shorts and sports bra. After grabbing my gym bag, I ran to the kitchen and got a protein bar. A quick check of my watch revealed thirty minutes until the fight.

As long as I didn't get caught in traffic, I'd have fifteen minutes to spare.

With the protein bar in my mouth and my bag over my shoulder,

I pulled the door open and stepped onto the porch. While locking the door, something right beside the door caught my eye. I turned to the side.

Flowers.

A vase filled with roses sat on the side of my porch. Beneath the vase, an envelope. Filled with excitement, I slid the vase to the side. On the outside of the envelope, a name was written in pen.

Jaz.

I checked over each shoulder and carefully opened the envelope.

On the outside, the card simply said *thank you.* I opened it. Inside, there was a small paragraph, written very neatly and with perfect penmanship.

Jaz,

Thank you for giving me a chance. I'll do my best not to disappoint you, and I hope so far I haven't done so. If so, accept these flowers as an apology. If not, accept them as a gift expressing my appreciation for you allowing me into your life.

Good luck tonight.

Ethan

I read it twice and then picked up the flowers and buried my nose in them. The sweet aroma caused me to salivate and filled me with an odd warmth. For, at least at that moment, what I believed to be the first time in my life, I felt appreciated for simply being myself.

It was an exciting time. I'd never received flowers from anyone before. As much as I didn't want to leave them, I carried the vase into my apartment, situated them in the center of the table, and placed the card in my purse.

***

I could see the disappointment on Ripp's face as soon as I stepped into the gym. Standing beside the ring with his hands on his hips and his eyes locked on me, he looked angry and disappointed at the same time.

"You've got fifteen fucking minutes," he growled.

I tossed my bag on the floor and removed my shoes. "I'm sorry. I had to work, and it just went to fuck after that."

"Why didn't you answer my texts?"

Because I couldn't afford to pay for my phone, and it got turned off.

"I don't know where my phone is."

It was true. It had been turned off for three days, and I really didn't know what I did with it after they turned it off.

He shot me a glare. "If you're not going to take this seriously--"

I shook my head. "I am serious. So serious. I want this more than anything. I'm really sorry. I couldn't afford the extra gas from driving here five days a week, so I picked up an extra shift to help pay for gas and protein bars. And my phone? I don't know where it is, really. But it got shut off."

"Why?"

It seemed like a stupid question until I remembered that everyone didn't have the same financial concerns I had.

"I couldn't afford to pay the bill."

His dropped his gaze to the floor. "I'll pay your phone bill."

"No you won't," I said.

I finished lacing my shoes, grabbed my jump rope, and sighed. "I'll pay it as soon as I can afford to."

"I said I'll pay it."

"And I said *no*." I raised my hands to shoulder height. "Sorry, I've got to warm up."

I began jumping rope while Ripp stood with a concerned look on his face. As with most people who weren't, trying to understand the difficulties associated with being poor was impossible for him.

"Let me pay it and you can pay me back," he said. "I need to be able to get ahold of you. You're going to go places in this sport, Jaz. And you can't fuckin' get there if I can't get ahold of you."

I responded as I continued to jump. "I might…let you do…that. I can pay you…back as soon as…I get another shift…picked up. Maybe like two…weeks. It's…not cheap…though."

His eyes widened comically.

"Eighty bucks," I said.

"I think I can work somethin' out."

"Thanks."

He motioned toward my bag. "Toss the rope."

I stopped jumping and dropped the rope on top of my bag.

"Listen up," he said. "Remember, she fights unorthodox. And her left hook is her signature, so watch for it. She almost always throws it right after a clench, so don't spend much time in close with her. If you get caught in there, get out quick."

He's already told me everything about her, but it didn't hurt to hear it again. I nodded. "Got it, Boss."

"She's been fightin' amateur for three years, and she's got about forty fights. She's undefeated, Jaz."

He's failed to tell me that.

"What if I lose?"

"You plannin' on losin'?"

"No, but I'm just asking. What happens?"

"Nothin'. It'll just be a setback. Be tougher for you to be accepted in the pros for a while. If you keep knockin' 'em out quick, it'll get a lot of people to talkin', that's for sure."

"It makes a difference if I knock 'em out?"

He nodded. "Big difference."

"And if it's quick?"

"Huge difference. A late round knockout can be dismissed as a tired opponent or a lucky series of punches. But first round knockouts back to back to back? It brings a lot of attention and gives you a label."

"A label?"

He nodded. "They'll label you a bad ass."

"I am a bad ass."

"Prove it," he said. "Give me a good fight."

"What if I give you a first round knockout?"

"Not going to happen with this one, Jaz. She'll just feel you out in the first."

We'll see about that.

I shrugged. "You never know."

"Ripton! You ready?"

I turned toward the voice. The referee stood at the edge of the ring, leaning over the top rope.

"Coming in now," Ripp said.

I grinned. "Ripton?"

He pushed my headgear onto my head and nodded. "Michael Allen Ripton. Don't act like your name's Jaz."

After he put on my gloves and checked them for rips, I climbed in the ring.

101

"What is it?" he shouted.

I shook my head. "Just Jaz."

I hated my name. Who the fuck would name their daughter Beth? Even in school, most of my teachers called me Jaz, and it was how I signed all of my schoolwork. No one called me Beth but my father.

"Get in the ring, Just Jaz."

I climbed in the ring and leaned over the rope. "Wish me luck."

He poked my mouthpiece into my mouth. "You don't need it," he said with a laugh. "You've got mad skills."

FOURTEEN

JAZ

Day forty-three

Where a professional fight brings legions of fans and onlookers – all seated in bleachers or seats surrounding the ring – amateur fights do not. There is nowhere to sit, no screaming fans, and no recognition for the winner or loser.

The fight begins, takes place, and ends with no one other than the trainers of the respective fighters – and the few friends who may have gathered – knowing the outcome.

I met her at the center of the ring, tapped gloves, and turned to the referee.

"I want a good clean fight," he said. "No hitting on the break. No low punches or hits after the bell."

I nodded. She nodded. He tapped his hand against the lower band on my shorts. "*This* is low."

He did the same to her. "And *this* is low."

"Understood?"

We both nodded.

"Go to your corners and wait for the bell."

On my way to the corner, I noticed Ethan standing beside Ripp. On Ripp's other side, Kelsey stood with his arms crossed. It appeared he was chewing Ripp out for something. Probably Ethan and me being in the ring together.

Fuck.

The old man hated me and I knew it. I stiffened.

The bell rang.

Shari "Thunder" Rose didn't scare me. Forty wins and no losses meant nothing more than she got an earlier start on her career than I did. By no means did it mean she was better. We met on her side of the ring, and she did exactly what Ripp said she would.

Her fancy footwork, shuffling to the side as I approached, and leading with an onslaught of jabs each time I got close enough to touch her prevented me from doing much.

Frustrated, I continued to be the offensive fighter. Fighting someone who wasn't willing to stand and fight was one of my pet peeves. Each time, as soon as I was close enough to touch her, she would throw a quick series of jabs and quickly step away.

Stand still, fight me, you scared bitch.

After chasing her around the ring for what I expected was half of the round, I grew even more angry.

Talking through a mouthpiece is difficult – if not impossible – but I loosened my grip on it and gave it my best.

"Stand still you scared bitch," I hissed.

A response wasn't necessary. Her eyes said it all. She didn't like it. She stopped dancing around and threw a wild right hook that missed me by a foot.

"I'm gonna knock your ass out," I taunted.

She shook her head and threw a straight left. I leaned left and the punch swung past the right side of my face. While she recovered from throwing the punch, her left side was unprotected. I threw a hard right hook into her ribcage.

She responded with an uppercut, catching me on the chin. And, for the first time in my boxing career, someone caused me to go blind from a punch.

I shoved my gloves into her chest and pushed her off. My sight returned almost instantly.

God damn, you hit hard.

Snot ran from my nose and tears rolled down my cheeks. As ridiculous as it seemed to admit it, it was exactly what I needed. I felt myself fill with rage.

Angry and seeking revenge, I stepped forward. She began feeling me out with shorts jabs, trying to lure me in. Ripp was right, if I got in close and stayed there for any length of time, she'd try and catch me with a hook as I broke away.

And if she did, I'd be in serious trouble.

But there was no way I could beat her if I wasn't throwing punches.

I swung a wild right hook into her arms, attempting to clear them from blocking my target. I wanted a straight shot at her face.

She threw a left hook into my ribs, and I didn't even see it coming. I countered with an uppercut that fell short.

As follow-ups, we both swung left hooks at the same time, hers a narrow miss, and mine caught her on the shoulder, knocking her off-balance. I followed with a right hook to her ribs.

The shock expressed in her eyes was enough for me to know she didn't like what she was getting, but I wasn't in the ring to make her happy. A hard left hook into the center of her stomach made her eyes bulge, and the sound of the bell prevented me from going any further.

"Bitch!" I grunted as I turned away.

I stumbled to the corner and leaned down. Ripp pulled my mouthpiece and gave me a shot of water. "What the fuck are you doing? Trading punches?" he asked. "You can't do that with her. She'll knock your ass out."

I shook my head. "She hits hard as fuck."

"And what were you doing? Talking shit?"

"Uh huh. She wouldn't fight."

Kelsey stepped around Ripp and glared at me. "You a boxer, or a brawler?"

I didn't respond.

"I asked you a question, Spaz. Which is it?"

"A little of both, Sir."

He pushed Ripp to the side and looked right at me. Wearing striped sweats and a white tee shirt, he looked angry, tired, and surprisingly tough for his age. "Looks to me like you're a brawler. Going toe-to-toe with a girl like her will get you hurt. Now get that right heel off the fuckin' deck, you flat-footed little shit, and maybe you'll have enough power to hurt her."

"Forget you even know this bald headed prick for right now. Watch my right foot and my hips." He threw a demonstration punch, twisting his hip in an exaggerated fashion as he did. "As your arm extends, twist on the ball of your god damned foot like your putting out a cigarette."

"Yes, Sir," I said.

"You've got power, Spaz. Now go knock her arrogant ass out, I'm tired of watching you two dance." He slapped his hand against Ripp's shoulder. "Put in her mouthpiece in, Dummy."

Ripp shook his head and put in my mouthpiece. And the bell rang.

106

FIFTEEN

JAZ

Day forty-three.

I rushed to the center of the ring, and she met me with a hard right cross, missing my head by the thickness of a hair.

Oh, now you wanna fight, huh?

I threw a flurry of punches in response, showing her just how quick – and how powerful – I could be.

She stumbled back a step.

I didn't want to beat her, I *needed* to. For me to quickly advance in the sport, I needed to knock her out and get noticed.

I wanted the label, like Ripp said.

Bad ass.

I took one step toward her and swung an uppercut. The punch blew past her, and in anticipation of her countering with her signature left hook, I threw a right in hope of knocking it astray.

Her left didn't come, and my right caught her hard on the side of the face, causing her to stumble again.

My vision narrowed. All that mattered was that I stay on the offensive, continually bringing the fight to her. If I did, she could only react. An offensive attack on her part, at least during my attack, would be all but impossible.

The ring became small, and only what was right in front of me was all that was in my view. All of the background noise became dull and distant. My breathing and my heartbeat were the only sounds I could hear, and they were almost deafening.

She threw a right cross, missing me completely. Her left jab fell short.

I looked her in the eyes.

She seemed distant. Confused. Uncertain.

You're hurt, huh?

Well, hold still, I've got something for you.

I crowded her, pummeling her with everything I had. She provided nothing in response, unless stumbling into the ropes was her defense. While I continued to pound her mid-section and face with repeated rights and lefts, the referee stepped in.

He grabbed her shoulders and looked into her eyes. "Are you alright?"

She nodded.

Not for long.

I cocked my right hand. The referee released her and stepped away.

I shuffled my left foot forward, moved my right back slightly, and twisted my right shoulder back. Pivoting on the ball of my right foot just like the old man said, I lifted my heel and threw the punch hard, bringing the power of my chest first and pivoting my hips right behind it.

The punch hit her square in the jaw.

She flew into the ropes, sprung forward, and fell to the mat face-first.

I glared down at her.

If you know what's good for you, you won't even try to get up.

The referee rushed between us, turned her over, and looked down.

She didn't move.

He waved his arms over her.

The fight was over.

Fuck yes.

I'd beaten the unbeatable by a knockout.

With my hands held high over my head, and feeling like I was floating well above the clouds, I rushed to the corner.

Ripp was dancing some weird victory dance, and Ethan was waving his hands in the air cheering. I spit out my mouthpiece. "I did it. I knocked her out. I'm on my way to being a bad ass."

I had never felt so much pride in my life.

Ripp stopped dancing. "God damn, you dropped that girl like a bad habit."

I pressed my forearms into the sides of my head and pushed my headgear up. "Sure did."

"Great fight, Jaz," Ethan said.

"Thanks."

My eyes darted around the edge of the ring, looking for Kelsey. Thirty feet away, walking toward the offices, the back of his white shirt and his gray hair were unmistakable.

I didn't care if he liked me or not, I was at least going to force him to remember me. "Kelsey!" I shouted.

He stopped and turned around.

"Thanks," I screamed.

Without acknowledging what I said, he turned around, raised his right hand high in the air, and flipped me the bird.

I love you, too.

SIXTEEN

JAZ

Day fifty.

Ethan was fighting, and he assured me he was fighting to win this time. Ripp and I were watching it together, and it seemed he had his doubts in Ethan's ability to win.

"This kid Ethan's fighting is a beast," Ripp said. "He should have gone pro two years ago."

"Why hasn't he?" I asked.

"I think he likes hurting people."

Ethan stood in the center of the ring, taking instructions from the referee. I was excited to see him fight, and if his prediction was correct, I knew it might cause Ripp to give him a little credit. He predicted a knockout, and we placed a bet on it. If he lost, we weren't having sex for a week. If he won, he got to have sex, on my terms. If he knocked him out, he got the sex of his choosing. Hoping he wasn't mistaken about the knockout, I stood excitedly at the edge of the ring.

Ripp folded his arms in front of his chest and sighed. "I'd like to slap the shit out of Ethan's trainer. He's a fuckin' idiot."

"Why do you say that?"

"Fuckin' Brockman? Because he is," he said. "He's picked some fights for Ethan that he shouldn't have. Ethan's got a fucked up record

111

now."

I wanted to tell him the truth, but I was sworn to secrecy. "Well, maybe he can redeem himself tonight. We've been sparring in my living room."

He shot me a crazy look. "You *what*?"

I grinned. "Sparring. Ethan and me. Maybe he's picked up on a few of my tips."

"You're fuckin' kiddin', right?"

I shook my head.

The bell rang. "Good luck, Babe," I shouted.

Ripp glared. "Babe?"

I shrugged.

"You two are fuckin'?"

"Shh, the fight started."

Ripp grumbled something and turned to face the ring.

Ethan's opponent was built just like him. Tall, with long arms and covered in muscle, he looked like a lean version of Ripp. His head was shaved, he was covered in homemade tattoos, and he had a tuft of hair on his chin.

He and Ethan clenched in the center of the ring, and Ethan shoved him off, swinging an uppercut as they parted. The punch barely missed. Seeing Ethan fight was a huge turn-on, and even if he lost, there was no doubt I'd be so horny at the end of the fight that I wouldn't be able to make it until morning without having Ethan fuck me.

"God damn," Ripp said, still focused on the fight. "If that would have connected…"

His opponent came at him with a barrage of punches, connecting many of them to Ethan's mid-section. A right cross from Ethan landed on his opponent's eye, sending him stumbling.

"*This* is a fucking fight," Ripp announced excitedly.

Yeah, it sure is. My pussy's loving it.

"It looks like it."

With every muscle in his body taught, Ethan continued to swing power punches at his opponent, connecting half of what he was throwing.

"Ethan's a slugger. He's fast and unpredictable. If he could just focus," Ripp said. "He'd be a good fighter."

"You think he's a bad fighter?"

"He ain't bad, he just needs some direction."

Ripp no more than spoke, and Ethan connected a hard right cross in the face of his opponent, knocking him back several feet.

"Holy shit, he's got him on his fuckin' heels," Ripp shouted as the man stumbled to regain his footing.

Ethan advanced toward him, and as soon as he was within arm's reach, swung an uppercut directly into his chin. The powerful punch sent his head back like it was on a swivel.

The fighter's legs gave out and he fell down to the mat, hard.

"Holy shit. He ain't gettin' up from that," Ripp said.

The referee waived his hands over the unconscious fighter, signaling the end of the fight. The entire thing lasted no more than a minute and a half.

I was soaked.

"Great fight, Babe!" I shouted.

"Back to the Babe thing," Ripp said. "What the fuck's going on there? You two dating?"

I shrugged.

"You don't know?"

"I don't think we're dating. We're just hanging out. And fucking," I said with a laugh.

Ripp raised his hand between us. "I've heard enough."

"No fuckin' on fight nights," he said, his eyes still fixed on the ring.

"Excuse me?"

"You heard me. Sex'll make ya weak. No fight night fuckin'."

"It loosens me up."

"No. Fight. Night. Fuckin'."

"Fine."

Ethan went to his corner, and talked to his trainer, waiting for the other fighter to be able to stand up. So far, he had yet to get up on his feet.

"So, Ethan's trainer is a dumb ass, huh?"

"Sure is," Ripp responded.

"Why don't you train him?" I asked.

"Haven't got time." Ripp said. "But if he keeps fightin' like this, I might make time."

Ethan commended the challenger and walked to our side of the ring.

"Great punch," Ripp said.

"Thanks."

"Looked good. Keep that shit up, and you just might make a champion."

"Appreciate it."

Ethan locked eyes with me. "So…"

"So…what?"

His excitement was apparent. I wasn't sure if it was about winning the fight or earning the right to fuck me any way he wanted. "You ready to go?" he asked.

"Something going on I need to know about?" Ripp asked.

"We made a bet," I said.

Ripp cocked an eyebrow. "What was it? The bet?"

Ethan shook his head.

"It's okay, he knows," I said.

Ethan stared in apparent disbelief. "Oh."

I turned toward Ripp. "Ethan said he was going to knock the guy out. I didn't believe him. So we bet. Sex any way he wants it if he knocked him out. And, he knocked him out. So…" I shrugged. "I guess anything goes."

Ripp stared at me for a moment, shifted his eyes to Ethan, and then back to me. "You serious?"

I nodded. "Yep."

He looked at Ethan. "Step on her head. It's the best shit ever."

What the fuck?

Ethan chuckled. "What?"

"Head steppin'," Ripp said straight faced. He glanced in my direction. "Plug your ears, Jaz."

I scrunched my nose. "Seriously?"

He nodded.

I covered my ears with my hands, but not so much I couldn't hear. I focused on the two boxers sparring in the far ring and listened in secrecy.

While I watched the two men fight, Ripp began to explain. "Bend her over, like over the couch or somethin' low. Get behind her and, you know, start goin' at it. Then, lift up your right foot, stretch it up there, and step down on her head. Right at the base of where the head's attached to the neck, and just mash her head into bed or the couch or whatever while your cock's inside of her. Havin' your leg all stretched out like that'll get you in there real deep. And somethin' about havin' their head stepped on really turns 'em on. Then, while you're stompin' her head, just fuck the hell out of her. You'll both love it."

Holy shit, that sounds hot as hell.

"No shit?" Ethan asked.

"If I'm lyin', I'm dyin'. Best sex ever. My Ol' Lady loves it. I give her that shit about once a week. Hell, even Dekk fucks his Ol' Lady like that?"

"No shit?"

"Motherfucker, I already told you once. I ain't lyin'. Try it."

I was already soaking wet from watching Ethan fight. Now, thinking about having Ethan fuck me while he stepped on my head?

I. Was. Soaked.

I stared off in the distance, acting none the wiser while my pussy continued to remind me of what was to come.

"So you ready to go?" Ethan asked.

I continued to stare, my ears covered tightly with my hands.

"Jaz! You ready to go?" Ethan shouted.

I uncovered my ears and turned around. "Huh?"

"You ready?"

I was so excited to get home and try it I could barely contain myself. Hell, I was ready for him to stomp on my head right then and there, but I knew I needed to hide my excitement. "Yeah," I said in an apathetic tone. "Sure am."

Ethan jumped from the ring. "Come on, let's get out of here."

"Have fun," Ripp said over his shoulder with a laugh.

"He's going to step on my head and shove me full of cock," I blurted.

"How could that *not* be fun?"

Ripp's eyes bulged. "You listened?"

Shit, I said that out loud, didn't I?

"Sorry," I said. "It's just part of being a girl. We don't like secrets."

Ripp shrugged and laughed. "Have fun. I gotta get. I've got my own business to take care of."

"See you tomorrow."

"Hopefully not with a sore neck," he said.

"Can't make any promises," I said, motioning toward Ethan's shoes. "He's got huge feet."

"You know what they say about guys with huge feet," Ripp said with a laugh.

"I do," I said, craning my neck to the side as if it were sore. "And it's true."

SEVENTEEN

JAZ

Day fifty.

"You don't think he was kidding, do you?" Ethan asked.

I really didn't care. Kidding or not, *head stepping* was a great fucking idea, and I was disappointed that I hadn't thought of it before Ripp told us about it. "No. I'm sure he was being truthful, why?"

"I uhhm. I don't want to hurt you."

"Hurt me?" I narrowed my eyes and stared back at him as I unbuttoned my jeans. "I'll let you know if I'm in more pain than I can handle."

"You sure?"

I coughed out a laugh as I pushed my jeans down my thighs. "Yeah."

The intensity of my pussy's desire to have Ethan step on my head and fuck me diminished somewhat on the drive back to my apartment. It wasn't that I no longer wanted it – because I really did – but my once soaking wet pussy didn't seem to share what was left of my mind's sexual interest.

He pushed down his sweats and sighed. "Okay."

"I'm gonna need you to talk dirty to me for a minute," I said. 'Before we get started."

Kissing and sweet talk never really did much for me, but a good

119

dirty talker could take me from nothing to nympho in seconds.

"How dirty?"

Dirty talk was something we hadn't discussed, but our first – and only – sexual encounter was kind of an unplanned combination of boxing and fucking that just happened. There really wasn't the time – or need – for him to talk dirty to me.

Now it was a different story. Being talked dirty to during sex wasn't something that I necessarily *required*, but it sure seemed to help matters along.

Being a woman was difficult work. Trying to make sense of my pre-period emotions, my mind's need to have a man be rough with me during sex, and my constant – and often insatiable – desire to have sex, was close to impossible. In the end, I rarely understood my sexual self, I simply chose to embrace my odd yearnings as being part of who I was.

"Dirty as fuck." I pulled my tee shirt over my head and reached for the clasp of my bra. "Smash your mouth against my ear and tell me how you're going to step on my head and stuff me full of cock. And anything else you want to say, just make it dirty. You can come up with something, can't you?"

Standing in front of me completely naked, he shrugged "Yeah," he said in a somewhat derisive tone.

He wasn't very convincing, but then again, he wasn't much of a talker – and he was much less of a braggart.

"Well, get to it." I chuckled and tossed my bra on the floor. "I'm ready."

In a few quick steps, he was at my side with his hand on my neck, gripping it firmly. He positioned himself behind me, pulled me into his chest, and breathed against my ear. "I'm going to shove you so full of cock that you're going to remember it each time you sit down for the next week."

Fuck yes, that's it.

His mouth moved down my neck, dragging his teeth along my skin until he came to a stop right above my shoulder. He then bit into my flesh, sending shivers down my spine as he did so.

Holy. Shit.

He pressed his lips to my ear. "You want me to give you a little bit of my thick cock?"

I was soaked. I regretted ever doubting his ability to talk dirty to me. I mumbled my response, but it still didn't come easy. "Uh huh," I murmured.

"Too bad," he breathed into my ear. "Because I'm not giving you a little bit, I'm gonna give you *all* of it."

Dear God.

He'd done it. I was past primed, and stood on shaking legs. With his chest pressed against my back and his hand still firm on my neck, he pushed me toward the loveseat. As my legs came into contact with the front edge of the cushion, he forced my head down, causing me to bend at the waist.

I eagerly bent over, exposing myself fully to him and his wishes. His foot kicked against the inside of my feet, reminding me to spread my legs a little further, allowing his massive cock entry into my willing wetness.

I felt the tip press against my sensitive lips. As he slowly began to penetrate me, I inhaled a choppy breath. Then, he pushed himself deep, causing me to exhale sharply at the feeling of being filled completely with is girth.

"I'm going to stretch this tight little pussy of yours out a little bit so I can fuck it."

Please do.

He released my neck and gripped my ass in his hands, spreading it wide as he pulled himself from within me. I felt his thumbs on the onside of my thighs, right beside my swollen mound. With slightly more force, he spread me wider. Then, all of him came rushing in, one thick inch at a time.

I gasped.

After a few slow strokes of his long thick shaft, I felt myself approaching climax.

It couldn't be. It had only been a few minutes and a few strokes.

His hands spread my ass cheeks apart, and his cock stretched my pussy with each stroke. I felt the tip of his cock bottom out and lunged forward, sending my head into the back cushion.

A slight tingling began to run through me.

Fuck yes. Spread it wide.

He pressed his hand against the back of my head as he continued to fuck me. I felt his weight shift slightly, and his cock twisted inside of me. And then...

Oh. My. Fucking. God.

His foot pressed into the back of my head, forcing my face into the cushion of the couch while his cock found space within me that I had no idea existed. Whatever was happening was redefining sex as far as I knew it. The tip of his cock was in an all-new place, and I never wanted it to leave.

"Oh Jesus. Right. There," I gasped.

With his right thigh hovering over my back, and his left foot on the floor, it was similar to having scissor sex. The depth of his cock was insane, and the feeling was immense, yet extremely pleasurable.

His foot pressed into the base of my skull was the icing on top of the sexual cake.

Although it was exactly what I wanted, I felt helpless and small – like I was being fucked by a powerful giant of a man.

Grunts shot from his lungs with each stroke while he continued to fuck me. I moaned into the dense fabric, embracing the combination of pain and pleasure as one.

His hands released my ass yet his thick shaft continued to stretch me to new limits. In anticipation of where his hands would land next, I opened my eyes and attempted to catch a glimpse of him, only to realize doing so was impossible with his size 13 foot smashed into my skull.

Then, his fingertip found my clit.

He rubbed my sensitive nub feverishly while continuing to remind me just how much I enjoyed being filled with his massive girth.

All of the feelings of pleasure began to merge, and quickly came together as one. My entire body began to tingle. His finger circled my clit, his foot pressed against my head, and his cock pounded my soaking wet pussy.

I cried out into the room.

"Oooohhhh Fuuuuccckkkk!"

An orgasm of newfound proportion rushed from within me, somehow escaping through every ounce of my existence at once.

My vision blurred. My ears began to ring. My legs gave out.

And, miraculously, I was transported – body, mind, and spirit – to a place I had never known.

***

I looked around me. I was in my bathroom, in the tub with water running over me, and Ethan was peering down at me with a sudsy loofah in his hand.

"You came really hard. Kind of passed out," he said. "I carried you in here."

I felt terrible. "Did you come?" I asked.

He grinned. "Oh yeah. That's part of the reason you're in here. I uhhm. I pulled out and shot it all over your ass. And your back. A little in your hair, too."

"Good," I said. "As long as I satisfied you."

He rubbed the soapy sponge over my shoulder. "You're worried whether or not you satisfied me?"

I relaxed into the warm tub of water and nodded. "Yeah."

"You letting me be part of your life satisfies me, Jaz. Completely. All the rest? Everything we do? The sex, the goofing around, the meals, and the fighting? That makes each day with you seem like Christmas."

He didn't speak often, but when he did, it seemed to always make me happy. I splashed some water onto my face and smiled as my pre-period emotions got the best of me.

And I thanked God that Ethan was a part of my life.

EIGHTEEN

JAZ

Day fifty-three.

Running through the thoughts in my mind, I searched a handful of distant memories, most of which were faded, but recollections of my past nonetheless. I came up with nothing that could compare. Granted, my childhood wasn't a typical one, but despite my father's abusive hand, I wouldn't call it dreadful either.

"I think I like this place," I said, turning to look in each direction. "A lot."

It was morning, a few minutes after sunrise. The oranges and pinks from the rising sun – but not the rays themselves – peeked out through the branches of the trees, giving them an eerie glow. Technically, it may have been a few minutes before sunrise, I wasn't sure. I was certain of one thing, I had never seen anything so beautiful in all of my life.

After walking down a stone staircase for half of a mile along the edge of a rock formation, we stood at the base of a large pool of water. Surrounding us were thirty-foot high sheer stone cliffs that rose up to another elevation.

From that upper elevation, water cascaded down off of the cliffs, freefalling into the pool of water at our feet.

A natural waterfall, dependent upon rain and the river above, which just so happened to be full. In a 180-degree arc, the waterfall rushed, creating a sound unlike anything I could ever remember hearing.

According to Ethan, *Hamilton Pool* was one of Austin's main attractions, and would become quite busy with sightseers after mid-morning.

At least for the moment, it was ours.

"After I moved here, I used to come here and just sit and stare at it," he said.

I wanted to respond, but my mouth had gone dry. Almost overcome with emotion from witnessing the beauty of not only what was before me, but of Ethan's willingness to share something so special, I fought against my tightening – and increasingly becoming dry – throat.

It was hopeless. With the sun's rays now shining beyond the bases of the trees and illuminating the cascading water, I was on the verge of tears.

And I didn't show emotion.

At least not until I met Ethan.

I turned to him and nodded. I couldn't offer much more. He returned a grin. I scanned the horizon, attempting to comprehend the passage of time having created the magnificent sight, but all I could do was absorb its beauty and gawk in awe of it all.

It was providing me what I had always hoped the beach would.

Proof of God's existence. A place to dream. A location where none of the earth's ugly existed.

Natural beauty, defined.

I turned toward Ethan, hesitated for long enough to adsorb his image, and turned back toward the waterfall. Beneath the soles of my sandals, sand. I kicked off my shoes, and pressed my feet deep into the cool grains. I felt his hand grip mine, and I grinned, squeezing his in return.

Different than anyone else I had ever met, Ethan wasn't with me simply for sex. He was with me because he felt that I offered him something worth obtaining. He was right. I *was* valuable, and I knew it. I may not have had riches, or any material things, but I had me.

As far as I was concerned, no one on earth could compare to me. All I ever needed was to have someone open their eyes wide enough – and for long enough – to recognize my beauty.

I watched the water rush over the edge of the cliff and separate into countless droplets as it fell through the space between the rock cliff above and the water below. The suspended droplets reflected the sun's rays, making each and every one of them look like precious jewels.

I squeezed his hand in mine. My eyes welled with tears. "This is beautiful."

"Not as beautiful as you," he said.

As I watched the priceless gems of water rain down over the edge of the stone formation, I realized I wasn't the most beautiful person on earth.

But I was holding the hand of who was.

NINETEEN

JAZ

Day fifty-five.

I stood at the door with a knot in my stomach and a frog in my throat. While I considered turning around and walking into the gym, the door yanked open, scaring me half to death.

I jumped back and screeched. "Holy shit."

He gasped in shock. "What in the fuck are you doing, Spaz?"

I swallowed heavily. "Have you got a minute?"

He exhaled loudly and gave me a stern glare. "For what?"

I swallowed again. "To talk?"

"I've got a gym full of future millionaires. Each fuckin' one of them sure they're going to win the next championship. All they need is a god damned chance. No, I don't know if you're ever going to make it. No, I don't think you're the best I've ever seen. Yes, I think you can be beat, and if you don't remember what I told you, I think it'll come sooner than you think. I think you need to work out less, eat more, and listen to everything you hear."

He took a breath, pressed his hands into his hips and sighed. "Did I answer it?"

"No, Sir."

He turned around and walked toward his desk. "Five minutes."

The office was almost as large as my living room. Pictures of boxers, some in black and white, and some in color, adorned the walls from wall to wall. Most of the pictures included Kelsey, and his age range from what I expected to be the oldest photo to the most recent spanned about forty years or so.

Behind his desk, and larger than any of the others, a color photo – obviously a professional shot – of a fighter's punch impacting the jaw of his opponent. The photograph was taken at the instant the punch – a left hook – made contact. The jaw of the opponent was distorted and twisted. Kelsey stood at the side of the ring in the background, his eyes as wide as saucers, and his hands reaching for the sky.

I followed him toward his desk and studied the gold inlay in the lower matting of the framed print as soon as I was close enough to read it.

Dekkar vs. Brock

WBC Heavyweight Championship

The Knockout Punch

It was the guy everyone talked about. The one who owned the gym, Shane Dekkar. Obviously one of his championship fights, and considering the position of the photo in Kelsey's office, probably the first one he won.

"I like that picture," I said, tilting my head toward the print.

He sat down in his chair and sighed heavily. "Something you'll never get to experience. Winning a championship."

You rude old fucker.

"Why not?" I asked.

"Brawler's don't win. Brawler's get beat. You need to learn to take a punch, because one of these days, somebody's gonna nail you with one, and you won't know how to react. Hell, I could go on and on, but I won't. Why'd you darken my door, Spaz?"

I sat in the chair in front of his desk and sighed. "I don't have family," I said. "My mom died giving birth and my dad abused me, so I left as soon as I graduated high school."

He remained without expression, his eyes fixed on mine. I suppose he'd heard it all, and my sob story was just another version of every other boxer's tale who'd been in and out of his life over the years.

"So, I really don't have anyone to ask questions," I said with a shrug. "There's a girl at work, and then there's Ripp, but I can't ask those two *everything*. So, I'm here for some advice because I know you won't go blabbing to everyone."

He leaned away from the desk folded his arms in front of his chest. "Boxing advice?"

"No, Sir. About life."

"I'm all fuckin' ears," he grunted.

Despite his attitude, I found it just as easy to talk to him as it was to talk to Freddy when I was young. "What do you know about love?" I asked.

His eyes glistened a little and he grinned. He instantly fought against the smile, pursing his lips until his stern appearance returned. He gazed beyond me and nodded his head slightly. "Close the door."

I got up and closed the door, grinning as I walked toward it. When I turned around, I wiped the smile from my face and sat down.

"What do you want to know?" he asked, still emotionless for the most part.

"First, I'm not in love. I know that much. But how do I know who's the right one? I used to think I was in love with a guy from a few years back, but now? Looking back on it, I'm not so sure. Not anymore."

He unfolded his arms and raised his right hand to his chin. "Prospective lovers are like hamburgers."

The comparison seemed ridiculous. My forehead wrinkled. "Hamburgers?"

His eyes narrowed to slits. "You gonna let me talk, Spaz?"

My eyes fell to his desk. "Sorry, Sir."

"Yes, hamburgers. You know, I used to get a burger over at 4th and Madison when I was a kid. At Stoney's. Best fuckin' burger in the world. I was sure of it. Lived my life until I was about twenty thinkin' that burger was the best. Hell, people used to ask me. They'd say 'Kelsey, where's a man get a good burger?' I'd tell 'em. 'Get your ass over to Stoney's at 4th and Madison. Best burger in the world.'"

He paused and shook his head. "When I was twenty-one, right before I fought that Irish kid from Philly, I got a burger at this joint in Atlanta. Name of the place was Fat Freddy's. Wasn't expectin' much, having had the best burger on the planet already, but I went in anyhow. It was some time ago, but I was pretty shocked at the price. Thirty-five cents for a burger was a hell of a lot back then, especially considerin' Stoney's were a quarter. I paid the price and waited while the guy cooked it right in front of me on one of them grills that runs the length of the counter. He was wearin' one of them little white hats like they used to wear. He handed me the burger, and I grunted him a 'thanks', pissed about the thirty-five cents. Anyway. I sat down at the bar with my malt and that 35 cent burger, wondering just how tough that Irish kid was gonna be. About the time I decided it didn't matter, I bit onto that burger. Well. Spaz, guess what?"

I shrugged, still confused about the comparison between hamburgers and love. "No good?"

"It was divine. I was in hamburger heaven. All that time, I was thinkin' Stoney's was the best burger in the world, and it wasn't. Fat Freddy's was. Hell, up until 1974, I used to drive from Austin to Atlanta just to get one of them burgers. That's the damned truth."

I didn't know what to say, so I just acknowledged his story with a "Huh."

"Well, 1975 rolled around, and I was workin' as a trainer at the time. Kid by the name of Joe Jackson asked me if I liked burgers. I told him I did, and I invited him to ride with me to Atlanta someday. He laughed at me right then and there. Said to me, 'why ride to Atlanta when the best burger in the world is at Dan's Hamburgers over on Lamar?'"

He shrugged and shook his head. "So, me and Joe took a ride to Dan's. I ordered the #2 – a double burger with grilled onions, mustard, and cheese. Waited fifteen minutes, them bein' as busy as they was. Well, the burger finally came, and it was wrapped in the paper that turns see-through when it gets greasy. That was the first sign. Same damned paper that Fat Freddy's used. I bit into that burger with a biased mind, Spaz. You know, with me bein' sure fat Freddy's was the best burger in the world. Well, one bite into it, and my mind was changed. All this time, I was thinkin' it was Stoney's only to learn it was Fat Freddy's, and then the year before the bicentennial, I find out the best burger in the world is right down the street, under my fuckin' nose, at Joe's."

"My point's this: searchin' for the perfect love is like searchin' for the perfect burger. You just need to realize that there's always somethin' out there – somewhere – that'll rival what you got. Hell, maybe it'll beat it. But if it was good enough to gather your attention in the first place, it ought to be good enough for the long haul. You just got to be smart enough to realize that different isn't always better."

He nodded his head and crossed his arms, obviously convinced he'd made his point. It was a good story, and it was well thought out, but it wasn't exactly what I was wanting to hear.

"How do I know the burger I'm eating is the right burger? The one for me?" I asked.

"Can you eat it for the rest of your life without eatin' another burger?"

It didn't take me long to answer. "I don't know."

"Well, find some time to go without it for a while. See if your mind tells ya to go grab another burger, or if you have a hunger for that burger you've already got. If you crave the one you have now, it's the burger for you. When you reach that point, you just got to understand, stop lookin' for somethin' better."

I grinned and nodded. "Okay."

He stood up. "Anything else?"

I shook my head and stood. "Nope."

"Big fight comin' up, you know," he said. "Girl's got one hell of a record. Beatin' her would be a ticket to the show."

"Me?"

"No," he grunted. "The other boxer in the room. Yes, you, Spaz. You listen to what that dummy tells you, you hear me?"

I guessed the dummy was Ripp, but asked anyway. "Ripp?"

"No, the other dummy trainin' ya," he growled. He lowered the tone of his voice. "He's a good kid, pay attention to him."

"I do."

"You better," he grunted. He pointed toward the door. "Shut the door behind ya."

"Yes, Sir," I said.

I considered what he said about the hamburgers as I walked toward the gym, and decided he was probably right. As far as I was concerned, there wasn't a better tasting burger on earth than the one I was eating. I guessed I just needed to decide if I was comfortable eating it for the rest of my life.

And, although I loved how it tasted, I wasn't completely convinced yet.

TWENTY

JAZ

Day fifty-nine.

It was the day before the fight. I'd been in the ring for almost an hour, and I was exhausted. I was barely able to lift my arms, and my legs felt like rubber. I knew what Ripp was trying to do, he was attempting to break me, preparing me for the *fight of my career* from what he said.

The problem, *his* problem, was that I'd keep going even if I had to hit the mitts while standing on my knees. I might have been a lot of things, but one thing I wasn't was a quitter.

"Right to the head."

I swung my right into the mitt.

"Left to the body."

I swung a left hook.

"Right," he barked. "Again. Again. Again."

I pounded the mitt, wondering if at some point I'd just collapse. Soaked in sweat, and bouncing on my toes in a puddle of sweat, I felt like I'd lost ten pounds, and I didn't have ten pounds to lose. Maybe Kelsey was right. Maybe I worked out too much and ate too little.

"Again," he snapped.

I pounded it again.

"Left, right, right."

I pummeled the mitts as hard as I could.

"Stop!" he shouted.

He lowered the mitts. "God damn, Jaz. You've got stamina." He glanced at his watch. "Hour fifteen straight. Most men would have quit thirty minutes ago. Maybe sooner."

I braced my gloves against my knees and tried to catch my breath, hoping he wouldn't ask me to continue for at least a few more minutes. "Drink, Boss?"

"Hell yeah, my bad," he said, reaching for the water bottle at the edge of the ring. He squirted a drink into my mouth. "So this girl's fought damned near a hundred and fifty times in seven fuckin' years. That's damned near one every two weeks straight for seven years. Her total record is 112 wins and 34 losses. Most of her losses are early, and with the trainer she's got now, she ain't lost one fuckin' bout. Seventy wins in a row."

I stood up straight. "Sounds like a good fight."

He scrunched his brow and shook his head. "You're her last fight before she goes pro. She's already got offers for some pretty big fights. Win or lose, you'll get some fuckin' attention. But I don't want you all down and depressed when she beats ya."

"*When* she beats me?" I snapped. "Don't you mean *if*?"

"She'll beat ya."

She'll die trying.

"Why do you say that?"

"112 and 34, that's why."

"Pfffft. That doesn't mean shit. She hasn't fought *me* yet."

"You're right," he said. "She hasn't. But you need to be prepared to lose."

He was wrong. I needed to stay positive. His talk of my certain loss was making me mad as fuck, but I didn't want to be disrespectful. "*She needs to be. Why won't you give me some credit?*"

"I give you credit where and when it's due. You're a damned good fighter, but like Kelsey said, you're a brawler. The tougher the fight gets, the tougher you get. Going up against a true fighter, you're an easy target to beat. A slow steady fighter will get you on points every time. A strong fighter will beat you by knocking you out long before you get mad enough to fight, and another brawler will be hard to find. This girl's a boxer. A damned good one. She'll be tough to beat," he said.

It pissed me off that he didn't think I was a good boxer. I realized I was under the impression I was a pretty good fighter, and it was hard to give myself an honest critique, but I truly believed I was pretty damned good.

I was sure I had more heart than almost anyone, and that had to be worth something. "I've got a lot of heart," I said. "More than any other girl in the ring."

He nodded. "I'll give you that much."

"It's worth something," I said.

He tossed the mitts onto the floor. "Just remember, no fucking on fight night. And, if something happens, and you just so happen to catch her on a bad night, the win'll get you a shot at the pros. People are already talkin' about that Thunder Rose win. So, another, especially against this girl? Well, they'd really be talkin'."

"What if I knocked her out?"

He shrugged. "Bad ass."

I wanted to prove him wrong. Freddy used to tell me I had to *earn* all the respect I ever got, and that no one *gave* respect. I needed to not only beat this girl but to knock her out. Then, I'd earn Ripp's respect.

I pounded my gloves together. "I'll give it my best, Boss. It's all I can do."

"Can't do better than that," he said. "And, just so you know, the champ is gonna watch the fight."

I wrinkled my nose. "The champ?"

He nodded. "Dekk."

Shit. The thought of him watching my fight made me nervous. He was all anyone at the gym talked about, and he was a local legend. Hell, he was the Heavyweight Champion of the World, he was a *global* legend.

"Why's he coming?"

"Comin' to watch her."

Makes sense.

"Oh."

"Alright," he said. "Hit the showers. And like I said, no fight night sex."

Whatever.

Fucking Ethan before the fight would settle me down, and make sure I fought a good fight, but I wasn't about to tell Ripp that. Boxers and their stupid superstitions. I didn't believe in any of them. I didn't need lucky charms, a certain amount of wraps in my tape, or to lace my boots a particular way to win a fight. All I needed to do was have a clear mid, remember what Ripp taught me, and give it my all.

"You got it, Boss," I said.

And I hit the showers.

TWENTY-ONE

JAZ

Day sixty.

With the rhythm of a dancer he gyrated his hips, bringing the pleasure of his thick cock with each well-timed movement. On my back with my heels high in the air, I mentally embraced each powerful stroke.

I craned my neck and looked at the alarm clock. "Five minutes!"

He lifted his head. "What the fuck?"

The fight started in thirty-five minutes, and the drive would take fifteen. Time wasn't on my side. "I can't be late," I said dryly.

The movement of his hips stopped and he shot me a look. "*You* can't be late and *I* can't keep having you barking out time limits. It's fucking me up."

"Alright, I won't say anything for ten more minutes." I said. "Now, get back to work."

Hovering over me with his hips wedged between my inner thighs, he flexed his chest muscles and glared. "What?"

I wagged my eyebrows and grinned.

He cleared his throat. "Get back to work?"

"Uh huh."

He pulled himself from inside of me and flipped me onto my stomach. The change was fast and unexpected. I was really enjoying our previous

141

position, but before I had time to protest, he shoved me full of cock.

I heaved out a breath.

Jesus.

"Get back to work, huh?" His hand came down hard against my right ass cheek.

Fuck.

The unexpected slap startled me. With my butt burning from the pain and my mind closing in on sexual euphoria, I shut my eyes and bit against my lower lip.

He began to fuck me like he was working against the clock. I guess in some respects he was. After each three or four strokes, his hand would slap my ass again, providing me a painful yet pleasurable experience. He repeated the process over and over, his rhythm becoming steady and foreseeable.

I closed my eyes and separated myself from everything except his predictable movements. Lost in the magic of being one with Ethan, my mind drifted away. My concerns about the fight, finances, and my fear of commitment vanished.

Encompassed in my bubble of bliss, I became lost. Separated from the often abusive world of reality, my fears, my past, and the worries associated with my future all drifted away and I began to tingle from head to toe.

Although my thoughts and feelings appeared to be lucid, I wondered if somehow my mind had become stuck between what was real and what was imaginary. The tingling from within me rang throughout my body like an electric shock, and I opened my eyes.

The orgasm caused my muscles to spasm. My entire body shuddered in response. I stretched my mouth open wide, wanting desperately to cry out, but doing so was impossible. With wide eyes and a warm heart, I allowed the tremors to run through me until they diminished to nothing.

The room smelled like sex with a spritz of Ethan's cologne. I rolled onto my back, closed my eyes, and inhaled the wonderful scent.

I opened my eyes. "Oh. My. God. That was intense."

Still catching his breath, Ethan grinned. "Agreed."

I glanced at the clock.

Fuck!

"Oh my God! The fight starts in thirteen minutes!" I screamed.

"Grab your bag." He jumped from the bed and grabbed his jeans. "I'll get you there in time."

It was a fifteen-minute ride to the gym, and it'd take a few more to get inside, to the ring, and geared up. There was no way.

Fuck.

"There's no way we'll make it."

"Grab your shit, Jaz," he demanded, pointing at my bag.

"I said I'll get you there, I'll get you there."

I rolled off the edge of the bed and attempted to stand. My legs — exhausted from the orgasm of epic proportion – folded beneath me.

And I fell to the floor.

TWENTY-TWO

JAZ

Day sixty.

"God damn it. You two idiots are makin' me look like a fool. Gimme your fuckin' hand," Ripp growled.

Ethan shoved his hands into his pockets. "Why?"

Ripp grabbed Ethan's wrist, pulled his hand from his pocket, and raised it to his nose. "You smell like fuckin' pussy."

He turned to me and shot me a laser sharp glare. "Did you fuck him? Is that why you're late? Don't fucking lie."

I didn't want to disappoint him, but there was no way I could tell him a lie. I swallowed hard and gave an almost indiscernible response. "Yes."

His eyes narrowed even more. He was fuming mad.

"But I was late because of a leg cramp," I explained. "He had to carry me to the truck." It wasn't the *entire* reason I was late, but at least it was true.

He turned toward Ethan, stared, and then shifted his glare back to me. After a few very intense seconds, he tossed his hands in the air. "Get her gloves and headgear on her, kid. You can help her through this one, I'm done."

Shit.

"No. I'm sorry. I'll…"

"You'll what?" he asked. "You're supposed to listen to your trainer, right?"

I nodded. "Yes."

He pressed his hands against his hips. "Follow his instructions?"

"Yes."

"Did I tell you no fight night fuckin'?"

I sighed. "Yes."

"And you fucked anyway, didn't ya?"

I sighed again. "Yes."

"Ripton, is your fighter ready?" the referee asked.

"I don't know," Ripp responded. He motioned toward Ethan. "Ask him."

The thought of fighting without Ripp as my trainer was gut wrenching. I felt terrible for disappointing him, and wished I could do something to fix it.

"She'll be ready in a minute," I heard Ethan respond.

"Please," I begged. "I swear. I'll do whatever you say."

His jaw muscles tensed. "If you make a fool of me again, I swear, I'll…"

"I won't."

"Ripton!"

"We're comin," Ripp snapped back. He turned toward Ethan. "Gimme those gloves, dip shit."

Ripp snatched the gloves from Ethan's grasp, and within a few minutes, I was ready to fight.

Ripp slid the headgear down, pounded his fist on the top it, and gripped the sides of my head in his hands. He held my face firmly and looked me straight in the eyes. "Disappoint me? I'll get over it. Disappoint yourself? Hell, I don't give a fuck. But him?"

He twisted my head to the side. Twenty feet or so behind the ring, the man from the picture in Kelsey's office stood with his hands shoved deep into the pockets of a hoodie. The Heavyweight Champion of the World, and he was looking right at us.

I swallowed hard at the thought of him being present for my fight.

"Don't disappoint *him*," Ripp said. "He owns this fucking joint, and he makes dreams come true for anyone willing to fight hard enough to fuckin' achieve 'em. Now get your skinny little ass in there and show him what you're made of."

I pounded my gloves together, eager to begin. "Box her or brawl her, Boss?"

"Get in there and box, Kid," he said.

He released my head, clenched his hand into a fist, and held it at arm's length. I pounded my glove against his fist.

Win or lose, I'll make you proud.

He slipped in my mouthpiece. I turned toward Ethan and grinned. He mouthed the words *good luck*, and lifted the bottom rope for me. Nervous, but for some reason feeling rather confident, I climbed into the ring and walked toward the referee.

He exchanged glances between us. "Touch 'em up."

We pounded our gloves into one another.

"You're going down no-name," she whispered.

I cocked my hip. "Excuse me?"

The referee pressed his hand into each of our shoulders, separating us. "There'll be none of that."

He turned and glared as me.

147

I glared beyond him and locked eyes with her. *No-name? I'll make you remember it, you fucking bitch.*

His eyes narrowed to slits.

I met his gaze, grinned, and nodded.

He looked at her. She grinned and nodded.

As the referee talked, I didn't focus at all on him or what he was saying. Instead, I glared at her the entire time. She returned my stare, but in her eyes, I saw a glimmer of what I hoped was uncertainty.

She may have fought a hundred and fifty fights, but she hadn't fought me yet. If she planned on beating me, I'd make sure she at least remembered my name for the rest of her miserable fucking life.

Get ready, bitch. When that bell rings, I'm coming and I'm coming hard.

The referee directed us to our corners. I went to mine, turned to face her, and pounded my gloves together while I waited for the bell to ring. All of the sounds outside the ring faded away and she became my only focus. Eventually, the only remaining sound was that of my beating heart.

Ding!

TWENTY-THREE

JAZ

Day sixty.

She met me in the center of the ring, and unlike the previous two fighters, she had no interest in a slow start. Her punches were quick and they came one right after the other.

I went to her with everything I had. After a series of body shots, I hit her with a three-shot combination followed up with a hook to the head that didn't connect.

Each time, she'd counter with a punch that came close to dropping me to the mat. The only thing that kept me on my feet was a little bit of stupidity and a whole bunch of stubborn.

Think, Jaz, think.

"The harder you hit, the harder your opponent will counter. Mix it up, light, hard, light hard. Then, catch your challenge right after she's hit you light, and let her have it."

I focused on my breathing and tried to slow my pace slightly. She stepped in close to work my body, and I let her. With my elbows tucked in tight, I took everything she had to offer. In return, I reluctantly followed Ripp's instructions and threw a few light punches.

Her next few punches into my upper arms and face weren't near as powerful as before. After countering with a few light jabs, I cocked my left, and threw a hook to her ribs with every ounce of my being.

The punch connected hard, and she winced in pain.

Fuck yes!

I felt like celebrating, but knew I was one punch into what was going to be a very long fight.

"Throw your hooks short, and your jabs long."

I threw a long right as if I was trying to hit someone fifty feet away. The punch glanced off the side of her jaw, but let her know I was in it to win it.

She came back with a hook I didn't even see coming, and caught me hard on the chin. My vision blurred, my ears rang, and I felt my legs go weak.

Fuck.

"When you're in trouble, keep your hands high and your elbows low."

I raised my hands to protect my face and hoped to regain my senses quickly. Her gloves pummeled my forearms, pounding them into the sides of my face.

"Don't let her finish punching before you start. Trading punches is for fools and show-offs, not for a talented fighter."

While she continued to pound against my arms, I swung a hopeful uppercut. The punch was wild, and didn't connect, but it caused her to step back and give me some much needed space.

She was a seasoned fighter, and Ripp was right. Boxing her was tough, and whatever I went to her with, she was prepared to counter. I was a good boxer, but she seemed to be a great boxer.

There was only one way to win against a girl like her and that was to *beat* her. The only way to beat her would be to lure her into an absolute slugfest.

A brawl.

She swung a wild right and I countered with a right hook. Both punches missed, and she came at me with a combo to the body that reminded me why I needed to do 500 sit-ups a night.

By the grace of God, the bell rang before she got another power punch unleashed.

I stumbled to the corner feeling like I needed a new plan of attack. Trying to box this girl was getting me nowhere.

Ripp pulled my mouthpiece. "She's killing you, Jaz."

I inhaled a deep breath. It didn't take a ringside commentator to realize I was losing. Hell, I knew it all too well.

"I know it," I said. "And what am I going to do to stop it?"

"Catch your breath, and we'll come up with a plan."

I glanced around the ring. Ethan stood beside the champ while he talked to Kelsey. I imagined the were reminiscing about all of the championships they'd won. Frustrated, I shifted my focus to my opponent's corner. Her trainer appeared to be giving congratulatory comments.

I wasn't prepared to lose. But I didn't want to box her for one more round.

Kelsey's raspy voice caused me to turn toward Ripp.

"Listen up, Spaz."

I turned around. "Yes, Sir?"

"You a boxer, or a brawler?" he asked.

"A little of both, Sir"

"Bullshit," he hissed.

I haven't got time for your bullshit, Old Man. I've got to figure out a way to win this fight.

I sighed. "Boxer, Sir."

"Don't lie to me," he growled.

I looked at Ripp. He shrugged and motioned toward Kelsey with his eyes.

Kelsey folded his arms in front of his chest. "I haven't got all fuckin' night to argue. Are you a boxer or a god damned brawler?"

I cleared my throat. "Brawler, Sir."

"Well quit fucking boxing, and get to brawling, you dumb little shit. And while you're brawlin', don't forget the body, Spaz. It'll wear her down and you'll get a clear shot at that head of hers when she's unable to defend it. The body first, always," he said.

He turned and walked back toward the champ.

I glanced at Ripp. "Did you mean what you said the other day? That I was going to lose?"

He shook his head. "Nope."

I knew it.

"You didn't?"

He shook his head, grinned his cheesy Mike Ripton grin, and raised my mouthpiece. "Show this bitch what's it like to get in a real fight, Kid."

Ding!

TWENTY-FOUR

JAZ

Day sixty.

I rushed to the center of the ring and swung a right hand to her stomach, then followed it up with a left hook to her ribs. Prepared for her to counterpunch with something significant, I clenched my jaw muscles and tucked my elbows in close.

She countered with an uppercut that fell short, and a right cross that didn't.

Her straight right hand caught me on the chin and knocked me senseless for a split-second.

Fuck, you hit hard.

I swung a right hook toward her head. The punch was too low and glanced off her shoulder. She stepped back and raised her gloves in front of her face as if she was going to let me exhaust myself. It was a common tactic for a boxer to allow his or her opponent to swing wildly for a long period of time, which would wear them out from throwing repeated punches with no period of rest. Then, the person who was previously being hit could advance, fighting against an opponent who was tired and weak.

A great idea except for one thing. I didn't get tired. Just like Kelsey said, I was a brawler. I would never win on finesse or beauty, but in my opinion, I'd never lose in an all-out fight.

I pounded her body and face hard with at least a dozen unanswered punches. I stepped back to get an idea of how she was going to react, and she came at me with a well-timed series of punches.

You're a tough bitch, aren't you?

I threw another combination of punches to her body and then her head, all in hopes of at least causing her to stumble.

Once again, she returned her own barrage of jabs, uppercuts, and hooks in response.

Jesus.

"Don't forget the body, Spaz. It'll wear her down and you'll get that head of hers when she's unable to defend it. The body first, always."

I stepped in close and worked her body hard. No differently than when I worked the heavy bag, I punched against her muscled torso until my arms felt like rubber, and then I punched her some more. Her counterpunches bombarded me, hitting me in the shoulders, face, and mid-section, but I didn't care. I was on a mission, and I wasn't going to let her stop me.

This type of fight was what I lived for. All I needed to do was outlast her. We were in a brawl, and if she thought for one fucking minute that she could beat me at my own game, she was sadly mistaken.

I wanted a shot at a professional fight, and if she was my ticket to the show, I was going to either beat her in all out slug-fest or hang up my gloves. I continued to pound her body, just like Kelsey said.

She, in turn, pounded my face.

Eventually, her arms got tired and she lowered her gloves slightly. It was exactly the break I had been waiting for. I had no idea how long she was going to need to recover, but I wasn't going to wait around and find out.

I swung a left hook into her ribs.

Exhausted from her non-stop attack on me, and from my two-dozen shots to her body, she folded up as soon as the punch impacted her stomach.

I swung a hard uppercut into the bottom of her chin, and she stumbled back a few steps.

I'm just getting started, and I'm not stopping until your ass in on your back, bitch.

I threw a hard overhand right that caught her right in the forehead, causing her to stumble even more.

Immediately, it was apparent that she was hurt.

Now fumbling to catch her footing, I knew if I could get in another hard power punch, I might be able to knock her down. She'd be humiliated if nothing else.

"Only throw your hard punches when you know you're going to connect them. Don't waste your power."

I bobbed my head back and forth and shuffled closer, making myself an elusive target as I approached her. She regained her footing and swung a wild left hook and followed up with an uppercut.

I easily dodged both punches.

As her glove swung by my face, I pounded her mid-section with a hard left hand and waited. The punch hit her hard, and the breath shot from her lungs like a rocket.

I looked for an opening, and she provided it. With her elbows held loosely at her sides, I knew one more body shot should open her up for the kill.

Sorry, but you're going to have to add one more loss to your record.

I swung a hard right hand into her stomach. Her gloves came down, completely exposing her face. It was a split-second opening, but my punches were lightning fast.

Everyone said the champion's signature punch was a left hook, so I thought there was nothing better for me to try if he was still watching my fight.

I swung my left with every muscle that I'd spent a lifetime honing. The punch caught her square on the jaw, knocking her head to the side like she'd been hit by a car.

Her mouthpiece shot from her mouth and she fell to the mat.

Hard.

As the referee ran toward us, I bent at the waist and hovered over her.

"I've got a name, bitch. Jaz Briscoe, don't fucking forget it," I growled.

The referee directed me to my corner. I paced the edge of the ring without taking my eyes off of her. He looked into her eyes and asked her a few questions. She stared back at him, looking as if she was drunk. He shook his head and waved his hands over her. The fight was over, and I'd knocked her out.

It was surreal.

I would have sworn the crowd cheered, the heavens opened, and the flashes from cameras were going off.

But I knew better.

For an instant, I was numb. When I finally snapped back to reality I rushed to my corner. Once again, Ripp was dancing his victory dance, Ethan, pumping his fist, seemed almost as excited as me. I scanned the edge of the ring for Kelsey.

He was nowhere to be found.

Excited and glad it was over, I ran toward Ripp and spit out my mouthpiece. I opened my arms. "We did it!"

"*You* did it. Never doubted ya. There ain't a fuckin' girl on earth that'll go toe to toe with you in a brawl. Kelsey and me been planning that deal for the last three weeks," he said.

I shot him a look. "Planning it? Seriously? That was a set up?"

He grinned and nodded. "Sure was. We knew you'd kill her in a brawl. Hell, you train for three hours without tiring out. The other night, Kelsey told me to keep you in the ring for an hour and a half and see if you'd give up."

I glared back at him. "Me? Give up?"

He shrugged. "We had to know. We just hoped you'd make it through the first round. Figured it'd take a round of boxing to you get good and mad at her. After seein' you train, both of us knew you wouldn't tire out, though."

"You fuckers," I said with a laugh. "Where is he? Where's Kelsey?"

"He had shit to do. He ain't much on celebratin'."

The entire experience had me close to tears. I was disappointed that Kelsey didn't care enough to stay, but still extremely pleased with winning. "Thanks for believing in me."

"It's easy to believe in a winner," he said. "Now go congratulate the loser."

I pulled my headgear and reluctantly walked to the other corner. Sitting down with her trainer and a medic, she looked pissed. I walked to her side, extended my right glove, and waited. After a moment, she extended hers.

I pounded mine into hers. "Jaz Briscoe, nice to meet ya."

"Amy Wilson. God damn you hit hard," she said.

I shot her a grin. "You too."

"Good fight."

"Good fight."

I ran back to the corner, and when I got there, the champ was talking to Ripp. Respectfully, I stood at the ropes and waited for them to finish. The champ turned toward me and gave me a half-assed grin.

It was almost as if he seemed nervous, but I knew better. He made a fist and extended his hand through the ropes. "Shane Dekkar. Nice to meet you, Jaz."

I pounded my glove into his fist. "Uhhm. Nice to…uhhm…meet you."

"You've got one hell of a left hook," he said. "I'd like to talk to you next week when you get time. About your future."

Still speechless, I glanced at Ripp. He grinned and nodded. I looked at Ethan. He seemed to be on the verge of becoming emotional. I shifted my eyes back to the champ and swallowed hard. "My future, Sir?"

He chuckled. "Call me Dekk. And, yes, Ma'am. Your future."

Still in shock from winning the fight, talking to the champion was almost enough to put me over the emotional edge. I muttered my response. "Uhhm…Okay."

He reached up and pulled the hood over his head and grinned a humble grin. "Have Ripp bring you by. Any time."

It was a hundred degrees outside. I wondered why he was wearing a hoodie, but didn't dare ask. "I will. Thank you."

"Again, nice to meet you," he said.

I stood with my mouth agape. "Uhhm. Same here. Thank you, Dekk."

He grinned and walked away, leaving me to wonder just what my future was going to entail.

TWENTY-FIVE

JAZ

Day sixty-six.

More than anything, I wanted Ethan to continue to be the person he was to me, but I was afraid there would be a point where he became like all of the others – eventually dismissing himself from my life.

I swallowed nervously and knocked. I'd been anxious the entire drive to his house, wondering why he'd asked me to come over. I'd never been to his home, and expected nothing good could come from the visit. Eventually, men always leave. I fully expected the time had simply come for him to do so.

The door opened.

Dressed in jeans and a button down, he looked handsome. His hair, as always, dark and scattered about his head in a perfect mess. He moved to the side. "Come on in."

I stepped inside, not knowing what to expect. The sweet smell of something baking caused my mouth to salivate and mind to drift away from thoughts of a disastrous ending to our relationship.

"Well, are you going to come in?" he asked.

I realized he was halfway down the hallway leading into the house, and I was still standing at the entrance.

"Yeah," I said with a smile, hurrying to catch up to him. "So what's

161

going on?"

The landscape crew he worked on had got off work at noon. Realizing he had come home from work, taken the time to shower and changed into the clothes he was wearing, I began to wonder exactly what was going on.

He glanced over his shoulder, grinned, and shrugged.

I followed him down the hall and into the kitchen. A long countertop separated where we were standing from the attached dining area. Beyond the countertop sat a small round dining table. On it, several boxes wrapped in fancy paper, a bouquet of balloons, and the source of the sweet aroma.

A cake.

I looked at him.

He smiled.

"Happy Birthday!" someone shouted.

Startled beyond belief, I spun around. Ripp and Kelsey jumped up from behind the countertop, each wearing ridiculous paper hats.

Confused, I exchanged glances between Ethan and the two paper hat wearing fools. "What…"

"Happy Birthday," Ethan said.

Even more confused, I shook my head. "But it's not my birthday."

"It sure is," he said. "June 6th."

He was right, June 6th was my birthday. I didn't realize it was already June, and furthermore had no idea how Ethan knew when my birthday was. Emotion quickly washed over me. I hadn't had a birthday party since I was a little girl. The last one I could remember, anyway, was when I was two.

"How…" My voice began to falter. I stood and stared, incapable of continuing to speak.

Noticing my emotional state, he wrapped his arms around me and held me close. "Ripp told me."

I bit into my quivering lip and turned toward Ripp. Wearing cargo shorts, sneakers, and his typical wife beater, he looked like a complete idiot with the cone-shaped paper hat atop his bald head.

He offered me the cheesy Mike Ripton grin and shrugged his innocence. "It was on the waiver you signed at the gym. Karen enters that shit in a computer, and it puts out a reminder. Kelsey told me, I told Ethan, and he decided to have a little party." He motioned toward the table. "Light the candles, Old Man."

Wearing his striped sweat pants, a white tee shirt, and the little paper hat, Kelsey looked adorable. He reached into the pocket of his sweats, pulled out a lighter, and lit the candles. He shoved his hands into his pockets. "Blow 'em out, Spaz."

I coughed out a laugh and fought not to cry. Ethan released me and followed me into the dining room.

I leaned over the cake and prepared to blow them out.

"Wait!" Ethan said. "We've got to sing."

And, the three most important men in my life sang Happy Birthday to me.

"Okay," Ethan said.

I closed my eyes, made a wish, and blew out the candles.

"Open this one first, I've got shit to do," Kelsey said. "I can't stick around this clusterfuck of a party all god damned day."

He handed me a long round cardboard tube with a bow tied around it, but it wasn't wrapped in paper.

"Okay."

I was still an emotional wreck, but seemed to be fueled by the excitement of actually having a birthday party. I studied the cardboard tube. On each end, a white plastic cap was pushed into the tube, securing the contents from falling out. Eager to find out what it was, I removed one of the caps and looked inside.

A poster.

I pinched the paper and carefully slid it from the tube.

"Be careful with it," Kelsey warned.

I nodded as I unrolled the large print, spreading it onto the countertop.

My throat tightened. My eyes welled with tears. I glanced at Kelsey. He nodded. I shifted my eyes to the print.

"Good fuckin' shot," Ripp said.

I couldn't cry. Not after everything I'd been through in my life without crying. Not now, and definitely not in front of the three men who stood before me.

I fought against the tightness in my throat and swallowed. "It…It uhhm." I tilted my head toward the print. "How…how'd you get it?"

"Hired a photographer. Surprised you didn't see the flashes goin' off," Kelsey said. "He shot a few hundred, but that's the one I picked. Damned good lookin' left hook."

The photo, taken an instant after impact, was of me hitting Amy Wilson with the knockout punch. My upper body was twisted, every muscle in my back was flexed, and my glove was slightly past her face. Her eyes, wide and glassy, expressed her concern.

There was one thing in the photo, however, that made me fill with more pride than winning the fight. Beyond the ring, standing next to Dekk, stood Kelsey.

With his hands raised high in the air and his mouth opened wide,

SCOTT HILDRETH

there was no denying the pride he felt for me winning the fight. A picture *was* worth a thousand words.

I rolled up the picture and slid it into the tube. "Thank you."

"Happy Birthday, Spaz," he said with a nod. "Now I've got shit to do. Ethan, thanks for having me."

He glared at Ripp, tossed his hat onto the table, and without speaking another word, left.

"Here," Ripp said.

I turned toward him. He handed me a box, wrapped with fancy paper and tied with a bow. I eagerly accepted it and carefully unwrapped it. A cardboard box, clearly marked with the insignia of the manufacturer.

Converse.

I glanced at Ripp and then at the box. I removed the lid. Inside, a pair of white and purple Ed Hardy Chuck's.

"How'd you know my size?"

"Got it off them raggedy fuckers in your gym bag. You need to toss them pigs in the trash. Stinkin' fuckers," he said.

I will," I said with a smile. "Thank you."

He folded his arms in front of his massive chest and nodded. "Happy Birthday."

One gift remained. A large box, approximately three-foot by three-foot square, and six inches thick, sat beside the cake. I glanced at Ethan. He nodded. "Open it."

"From you?'

"Yeah," he said. "Open it."

I inhaled a deep breath. "Okay."

I removed the bow, carefully removed the paper, and lifted the box. It was surprisingly heavy. Anxious to see what was inside, but not wanting the event to ever end, I reluctantly removed the lid.

A sea of purple silk.

I scrunched my nose and stared.

At least they know my favorite color.

I reached for the fabric, lifted the heavy garment from the bag, and held it at arm's length.

A silk boxer's robe, just like the champion's wore. I'd always dreamed of the day I would have my own. I imagined myself wearing one, jogging down the aisle while people reached out in hope of slapping my hand as I rushed toward the ring. With the crowd cheering my name, I would duck under the ropes and wave, only to have thousands of screaming fans wave back.

It was a dream for sure, but one I liked thinking of.

"Turn it around," Ethan said. "But don't get mad."

I shot him a playful glare. "I'm not going to get mad."

I turned the robe over and stretched the material wide. Across the back, in large gold letters, a name had been stitched into the purple silk.

BRAWLER.

My heart swelled. It was perfect. I draped the robe over the box, turned toward Ethan, and kissed him full on the lips.

On that day, the 6th of June, I turned twenty-five in the presence of one grumpy old fucker, my trainer, and the man I was quickly falling in love with.

And it was the best day of my entire life.

TWENTY-SIX

JAZ

Day sixty-eight.

We were sitting in Dekk's office at the gym, talking about *my future*. Eager to find out what was going to happen next in my career, I listened as he explained matters.

"There was some pretty heavy talk about Amy Wilson," Dekk said. "She was actually scheduled to go pro, and was expected to fight an undercard fight at a championship fight. But, no contracts had been signed yet."

"And now that I beat her?" I asked.

He shrugged. "She's still going pro, but they aren't asking her to fight on that card."

Ripp slapped his hand against my shoulder. "What are they sayin' about my girl, Jaz?"

The champ looked at Ripp. "Her knockouts have made some people talk. Beating Rose and then beating Wilson got a lot of people wondering just who she is and where she came from. That's kind of why we're here. I told Kelsey not to respond, but the promoters have been calling all day asking me."

Ripp turned to face the champ and put his hands on his hips. "Askin' you what? Quit beatin' around the fuckin' bush. You're all stammerin'

167

around and talkin' in fuckin' circles. Let's hear it."

Based on the way Ripp talked to him, it was pretty obvious they really *were* friends.

Dekk locked eyes with me. "Were you fighting amateur when you were in Omaha? *Officially*?"

I nodded. "Yes, Sir. I was boxing in *USA Boxing*."

It was a governed amateur boxing association that Freddy insisted I fight under so I could one day go to the Olympics.

"How many fights did you fight before you were seventeen?" the champ asked.

"I quit when I was sixteen. I don't know, I can't really remember. The younger years of my life are all foggy."

"Did you remain under USA Boxing's governing body for the entire time?"

I nodded. "Yes, Sir. I can remember that. Freddy, he was my trainer. He insisted that we fight *AIBA* so I could go to the Olympics. That was his dream."

"You're required to fight eighteen fights a year. Do you think you fought that many?"

"If it was a requirement, I'm sure I did. Freddy would have made sure of it."

"Do you have any idea how many fights you won?"

I grinned. It was an easy answer. "All of them, Sir."

His eyes shot wide and he coughed. He looked at Ripp. Ripp grinned. The champ looked back at me and smiled. "*All* of them?"

"Yes, Sir. Never lost one. That's why Freddy was so sure I could make it to the Olympics."

He stared back at me in apparent disbelief. "You're undefeated?"

I hadn't really thought about it, but technically I guessed I was. As far as I was concerned, my fights when I was younger didn't count, though. I shrugged. "I mean, I guess so. Do those old fights count?"

"They sure do," the champ said.

"I'll go to the AIBA and have your records pulled. They'll have them on file," he said.

"Okay," I said. My eyes darted back and forth between Ripp and the champ. "What does all this mean?"

"I'll tell you what it fuckin' means," Ripp said. "It means Ol' Dekk here can go to promoters and tell 'em that we've got a fighter here at Kidd's gym that's won a hundred fuckin' fights, and lost none. And, we can say she's knockin' bitches out left and fuckin' right, and she wants a shot at someone worth fightin'. Right, Dekk?"

The champ nodded. "That's right."

I smiled at the thought of it all. "Oh."

"Oh?" Ripp said sarcastically. "Hear that, Dekk? Sound like someone you know? Bunch of humble fuckers in here today, huh?"

"Humility will keep her grounded," he said.

Freddy used to tell me the same thing.

I studied Dekk. He didn't look like a champion, that was for sure. Dressed in shitty blue jeans and wearing a pair of biker boots and a hoodie, he looked like one of Austin's many homeless residents. Realizing he was actually the Heavyweight Champion of the World let me know that he was a very humble man.

I liked that about him.

"Yes, Sir. It sure will," I said. "Freddy told me that. He said I should always be humble outside the ring."

"He sounds like he was a great trainer. I tell you what, I'll have Joe get your records pulled. Once we get our hands on them, I'll let you know what we find out. But Ripp's right. If we can prove your record, we can make one hell of a claim to get you accepted into the pro circuit."

"And then what?"

"Your first few pro fights should get you noticed, especially if you can keep up that knock out record."

He stood up.

Ripp had been standing the entire time.

I stood and wiped my hands on the front of my shorts.

"Just out of curiosity," he said. "How many of your wins were knockouts?"

I shook my head. "Hard to say. From what I can remember, probably quite a few. It's just. I don't know. I just don't really remember the fights. I mean, I remember Freddy, and I remember fighting, but I don't *really* remember it. It's hard to explain."

"I understand," he said. "Believe me."

He clenched his hand into a fist and extended his arm.

I grinned and did the same.

And he pounded his fist against mine.

TWENTY-SEVEN

JAZ

Day seventy-one.

Ripp and I stood at the edge of the ring and waited for Ethan. The scheduled fight was with an undefeated fighter who was even more well-known than the last fighter Ethan fought. According to Ripp, if Ethan could beat the guy, his other than satisfactory record really wouldn't matter very much.

Defeating the two most recent fighters would outweigh all of his losses, and he'd gain respect in the amateur boxing circuit for being a noteworthy opponent.

I couldn't tell Ripp, but Ethan had once again told me he was going to win the fight. His prediction? Another first round knockout. For Ethan's sake, I hoped he was right.

"Can't wait to see what happens," I said.

"Shit, I can't wait to see what Dekk finds out about your record. I'm anxious about this fucker, too."

"I'm anxious about my *record*. I can't wait to see what he finds out. It's exciting to think about."

Several minutes passed without him speaking. It wasn't like Ripp. I studied him for a moment. He stood with his hands in the pockets of his shorts and his eyes fixed on the floor, rocking back and forth on the

171

balls of his feet.

"What are you thinking about?" I asked.

"Huh?"

I chuckled. "You look like you're either thinking or nervous."

"Me? No, I ain't nervous."

"So what are you thinking about?"

"I don't know. I guess I been wonderin'," he said.

"About what?"

"You can't remember anything about when you were a kid?"

It wasn't an easy thing to explain. I could remember some things, and not others. There was a long period of time from when I was about two until I was a sophomore in high school where I really couldn't remember anything specific about my life, only the bruises and how bad they hurt when I touched them. Then, after Freddy died, for whatever reason, I could remember almost everything.

"It's weird. I can remember it, but I can't remember specific things that happened. My counselor in high school told me it was pretty common for kids like me to repress memories, but he said it was odd that mine was the way it was. I'm really pretty happy with it the way it is, honestly. If I remembered everything, I'm sure I'd just be mad."

He pursed his lips and inhaled a deep breath through his nose. "I hate thinkin' about your pop knockin' you around when you was a kid. You think you'll ever try and reconcile things with him?"

It was a question I had never been asked, but was one that I was more than prepared to answer. I'd thought about it several times from when I was in high school to rather recently, and each time I came up with the same answer.

"No, I won't," I turned to face him. "If it would have happened once or twice in a drunken fit of rage, I could probably get over it. You know, forgive him. But it didn't. It happened over and over. So, what excuse can someone like him give for beating on a little girl with his fists? What could he say to make me forgive him?"

His jaw muscles tightened and his eyes fell to the floor. "Don't know."

"Yeah," I said. "Me neither."

"If you can't remember your childhood, how do you remember that, though?"

The answer was what I hated about it all. "Because that's really the only thing I *can* remember."

He looked up and nodded at the exact moment Ethan came from the locker room with his trainer.

Ethan looked ready for anyone or anything. He stared straight ahead and pounded his gloves together as he walked, his biceps flaring with each movement of his upper arms. There was no denying he was focused, and I was proud that he agreed to fight the man he was going to fight.

Dressed in his blue and white shorts and an old raggedy gray sweatshirt with the sleeves cut off, he looked like what I had always imagined the old school boxers from the gyms in Philadelphia looked like back in the day.

"Kick his ass, Babe," I said as they walked past.

Ethan's trainer glanced toward us, and Ripp glared back at him.

"What's the deal between you two?"

"Just don't like him," Ripp said.

It's apparent.

Ethan nodded, but didn't speak. His focus was clear.

"I'd like to see Brockman try and fight this guy. He'd probably get his ass kicked," Ripp said.

Ethan's trainer was almost as big as Ripp, but seemed to lack Ripp's intensity. "Why do you say that?" I asked.

"I think he's a fuckin' pussy."

"Was he any good as a fighter?"

"Nobody knows. Ought to have Dekk try and find *his* records," he said with a laugh. "Probably come up empty-handed."

The referee gave his instructions and then directed the men to their corners. On his way to the corner, Ethan met my gaze, raised his right hand, and grinned.

I clenched my fist, raised my right hand, and smiled in return.

Ding!

Ripp rubbed his palms together. "Here we go."

Ethan rushed to the center of the ring, greeting his rather large opponent with a few quick jabs. The other fighter countered with a few jabs of his own, and threw a powerful uppercut.

Ethan dodged the punch.

"God damn," Ripp howled. "If that fucker would have connected..."

With each punch that was thrown in his direction, Ethan bobbed his head back and forth, almost taunting his opponent. In response, he grew angry, swinging more frequently and rather wildly.

"Shit, Ethan's gonna lure this fucktard into wearin' himself out in the first round. Look at his dumb ass throwin' all he's got."

"I hope so," I responded.

Come on, Babe. Wear him down, and then give it to him.

I pointed at Ethan's opponent. "As soon as his gloves come down, Ethan going to give it to him."

"Kid's got a damned good sense of awareness. And nice defensive posture," Ripp said.

"Which one?"

"Ethan," he said.

"Make him come to you," I shouted.

"Good advice," Ripp said over his shoulder.

Ethan stepped back and raised his gloves. His opponent quickly shuffled forward, already clearly frustrated. With his right glove held lower than his chin, he seemed to be either out of shape, or preparing to throw a hard right hand.

As soon as he was within reach, he threw an uppercut. Ethan leaned back, and the punch flew past him. He countered with a straight right, which was exactly what he should have done. The punch connected well, and stopped his opponent from advancing further.

And then, Ethan threw an uppercut.

The uppercut.

The punch started with his glove at his thigh, and swung straight up into the chin of his opponent. A punch no man could recover from if it connected well, and it connected in a picture perfect manner.

There was no need for the referee to call the fight.

An official declaration wasn't necessary.

The fight was over, and the only one who didn't realize it was the man flat on his back at Ethan's feet.

"Fuck yes!" Ripp howled. "That's what the fuck I'm talkin' 'bout."

Ethan stepped to his corner. The referee called for a paramedic. After an extremely tense ten minutes, the man finally sat up and looked around.

We cheered as he stood up, grateful that he wasn't hurt much worse.

"That kid's got some fuckin' power," Ripp said. "You know what I think?"

I shook my head. "No, what?"

"I think Ethan needs a real trainer."

"You?" I asked excitedly.

He nodded. "Yep."

Oh my God.

It would make Ethan so proud to think that Ripp was willing to train him. Hell, it made me proud to hear him say it. I knew his time was extremely valuable, and other than me, he only had one other fighter he was working with. To have him work with Ethan would be a huge boost to his ego.

"Really?"

"I'm tellin' ya, all he needs is someone who believes in him *and* is able to give him proper direction. Brockman don't fuckin' know which fuckin' way's up. So. Yeah. I wanna get him under my wing and turn him into a champ."

"That'd be awesome," I said.

"Don't say anything to him," Ripp said. "I want to ask him."

"I won't say a word."

I felt better than I could ever remember feeling. *Ever.* Ethan had won again by knockout, and was going to be trained by Ripp, who he admired deeply. I couldn't have been more proud of him, and feeling that level of pride toward another person was something new to me.

Something new and very different than what I was used to.

It was all the proof required to convince me that I cared about Ethan deeply. What I had feared admitting no longer needed to be confessed. My level of pride proved to me how I felt about Ethan.

And it was time I let him know.

TWENTY-EIGHT

JAZ

Day seventy-nine.

Speaking to Ethan about my feelings was easy. I suspected it was because I felt that he wasn't going to reject me, laugh, or run away. "So, I've been thinking," I said.

He reached into the skillet with the spatula. "About?"

I watched him flip over the eggs. "Us."

"What about us?"

"I like this," I said.

He lifted the eggs from the skillet one by one and placed them on the plates. "Having me make breakfast?"

"No, dork. Well, I mean, yeah. But that's not what I'm talking about."

"What, then?"

When he slept over, I loved how it felt so perfect. In the past, I'd always felt like there was a time when I wanted my space. With Ethan, I didn't want *my* space. I wanted all the space that existed to be *ours*.

"Everything," I said. "I like everything."

"Me too." He handed me one of the plates and turned off the stove. "Life is good."

Men could be so aggravating. Trying to understand them was impossible sometimes. Succeeding at explain feelings to them was even

177

worse. "Life *is* good. But I'm talking about the space between us."

"What space?"

"I want it to be ours."

He sat down and took a bite of his eggs. "You want what to be ours?"

"The space."

"What space?"

"The space between us."

He swallowed his food and took a drink of coffee. "I'm lost."

No shit.

I rested my elbows on the table, pressed my palms together, and sighed. "I don't want my space back."

He sighed. "What space are you talking about?"

I slid my plate to the side and cleared my throat. "When you're gone, there's space between us. And. I. Don't. Like It."

He picked up his toast and took a bite from the corner. "Me neither."

Thank God.

I reached for my plate and grinned. "Okay. Good."

He took another bite of toast. "What are we going to do to fix it?"

"Not have the space."

He looked past me and narrowed his eyes while he nibbled on his toast. After finishing the entire piece, he took another drink of coffee. "As far as I'm concerned, there's never space between us."

It was the dumbest thing I'd even heard. "How can you say that?"

He pounded his fist against his chest. "Because you're always right here."

It was cheesy, but I loved it nonetheless. I puckered my lips and leaned toward him. He met me halfway and kissed me, leaving toast matter on my lips. I brushed it off and grinned, still feeling like I needed more.

"When you're gone? Like at work, or whatever? I think that's stupid."

In the middle of using his second piece of toast to clean the egg yolks, he looked up. His eyes were filled with confusion. "You think it's stupid that I work?"

"No," I said. "I think it's stupid that you're gone. When you come back it's okay. It's just dumb when you're gone."

He nodded like he understood, but I had my doubts. He poked the toast in his mouth, chewed it, and swallowed. After a drink of coffee, he leaned back in his chair.

"You're confusing me. Seems like you always do this when there's something important that you want to tell me. When you're *not* trying to tell me something I get much better information." He chuckled. "When you're on a mission, it's really tough to figure out what you're thinking. Can we start over?"

I fucking swear, men are so stupid sometimes.

"I don't ever want to be without you."

He took another sip of coffee and gazed in my direction. His eyes – and the look on his face – confirmed he felt the same way. "I don't ever want to be without you, either," he said.

It appeared we were on the same page. I took a deep breath. "I think I might be falling in love with you."

He started coughing, and it lasted until he stood up.

My heart sank.

Looming over me and attempting to catch his breath, he looked down and shook his head.

"Shit," he said. "I fell in love with you a long fucking time ago.

Where have you been?"

You did?

My eyes widened. "Really?"

He coughed a few more times, grinned, then nodded. "Really."

I felt warm. The all over kind of warm. I swallowed hard and stood up. "I might have done the same."

He spread his arms wide. "Let's make an agreement."

I pressed my tongue against the roof of my mouth and swallowed again. "Okay."

"What did you call it earlier? The space between us?"

"Uh huh."

"Let's just agree that we're always together in *here*." He pressed the palm of his hand against my boobs. Eventually, it came to rest over my heart.

My heartbeat increased tenfold. He smiled. I smiled in return. "Okay."

"If we do that," he said. "We'll never be apart."

Never apart.

It was exactly what I was after.

TWENTY-NINE

JAZ

Day eighty-two.

Ripp had called me to a meeting with Shane Dekkar to discuss what he found out from USA Boxing. Eager to find out what my record was and if we could use it in my promotions, I agreed to meet, but insisted that Ethan come along.

If Ethan was going to be included in my future, he needed to be included in decisions about my future.

With Ethan at my side, I knocked on the door.

"Come in."

I pushed the door open and peered inside. Kelsey and Ripp stood at the front edge of the champ's desk, laughing and talking. As soon as we stepped through the door, the talking stopped.

I couldn't help but wonder what they were talking about.

The champ stood up and extended his hand. "Ethan."

Ethan shook his hand.

He released Ethan's hand and shook mine. "Jaz."

I smiled. "Mr. Dekkar."

"Dekk, or Shane, please."

I grinned. "I like Dekk."

"Then call me Dekk."

"Glad that's settled." Ripp chuckled.

"Spaz," Kelsey said with a nod.

I rolled my eyes at him and positioned myself beside Ripp. "What did you find out? I'm guessing something or you wouldn't have called me, huh?"

He sat down at his desk. "As with all amateurs there's what actually happened, and what's *official*. They're never the same. Trainers, managers, record keepers, there's always messing with numbers. So, with you, all we know is what's official."

He reached for a folder, opened it, and met my gaze. "Care to guess?"

I shrugged.

"Ethan? You care to guess?"

I hadn't told Ethan anything about my previous record. Not telling him was out of respect more than anything, and for me to maintain a healthy level of humility. In short, I didn't want to seem pretentious or conceited about my career.

He shrugged. "I really don't know." He glanced at me, then reached for my hand. While holding my hand in his, he continued. "We haven't talked about it. She asked me to come to support her in making decisions about her future."

Dekk nodded.

"Just fuckin' say it. I swear. You and your beatin' around the bush bullshit. Tell her," Ripp complained.

"Wins, one hundred and thirty-two. Including the wins here at the gym, one hundred and thirty-five. One hundred and thirty-five *official* wins." He glanced at each and every person in the room.

My heart pounded. It was exciting to know the official numbers, although I suspected they would be something close to what he said. As far as I was concerned, it wasn't *that* impressive. I was young, and the girls I fought weren't as well-trained as me. I wondered how Ethan felt regarding everything. I began to feel guilty for bringing him. For his sake, I wished my record didn't have as many wins. I squeezed his hand.

He squeezed mine in return.

"Care to hear the losses?" Dekk asked.

I glanced at Ethan. He smiled. I looked at Dekk and shrugged. "Sure."

"Let me see if I can find it." He traced his finger along the surface of the paper. It came to a stop at a location out of view to all of us. "Oh, wait. Yeah, here it is."

He looked up. "Zero."

My heart raced. "Zero?"

He nodded. "Officially, *zero*. Officially, you're 135-0. Officially, you have a better record than I do. Officially, your record is one of the most impressive records out there. Oscar De La Hoya was 223-5 as an amateur. Kid Chocolate's amateur record was 100-0…"

"Donald Curry's was 400-4," Kelsey interrupted. "Amateur record, that is."

"The point we're making, Jaz, is this." He dropped the file onto the desk. "Your record is impressive. *You're* impressive."

I squeezed Ethan's hand. "Thank you."

"This information? It's public record. Anyone can obtain it. All they have to do is ask. I've taken the liberties to leak it out to a few people, and for good reason."

He looked at Kelsey and then Ripp. He inhaled a deep breath, held it for a moment, and exhaled. He fixed his eyes on me. "Do you know who Shay Simpson is?"

Ethan squeezed my hand firmly. I squeezed back. My throat tightened. "Shockwave? Shay *Shockwave* Simpson?"

He chuckled. "That's her."

Everyone knew who Shockwave Simpson was, even if they didn't follow women's boxing. She was on the news constantly. She was in movies, magazines, commercials, *everything*. When she wasn't in a fight defending her title, she was talking shit on whoever was preparing to fight her next. Her tasteless quotations were all over Facebook, Twitter, and Instagram. It was so bad that a #shockwave search on *Google* or *Twitter* would produce thousands of her ridiculous remarks.

"She's the champ," I said. "135 pounds of bad ass, that's who she is. Everyone knows her, she's on ESPN talking shit on people all the time."

Everyone laughed. Dekk inhaled another deep breath and then folded his arms in front of his chest. "How'd you like to fight her one day?"

"I'd love to fight her someday," I said excitedly. "Her, or someone like her. That's my dream."

"What if a chance like that came, oh, as soon as next month?"

I coughed out a laugh. "Yeah, right."

There was no way Shockwave Simpson would fight me. She fought women who had been in the pros for years, most of which she considered to be her rivals. She and her opponents bickered back and forth on Twitter, sending out tweets about each other, building up hype for the upcoming fights.

"Let me explain something," Dekk said.

"Can I sit down?" I asked.

He laughed. "Sure."

"Well." I pointed at Ripp and Kelsey. "Everyone's standing. I'm sorry, I'm just nervous."

"Nothing to be nervous about," he said. "We're all family here."

Shane Dekkar appeared to be the opposite of Shockwave Simpson. He was just a down to earth guy who happened to be a great boxer, and it was easy to admire him.

I counted the available chairs.

Three.

"Sit down," I whispered, pointing to a chair beside Ethan. "I'll sit on your lap."

Ethan didn't argue, and quickly took the seat. I sat on his lap and he wrapped his arms around my waist. I felt comfortable in his arms.

Protected.

I nestled in Ethan's lap and looked up. "Okay, I'm ready."

Dekk looked around the room. "Championship fights are more about money than anything. During training, there are times when either the challenger or the champion gets hurt. If that happens, their team keeps it quiet. A leak to the press of an injury will change the odds on the fight, and have a huge effect on the money bet – and potentially earned – in places like Las Vegas. But, people do get hurt. Typically, what happens – and we've all seen it – the injured party doesn't make an official statement until right before the fight. They wait in hope of the injury getting better, and when it's apparent it won't or can't, they claim injury and step aside."

It made sense, but I had no idea what it had to do with me. If he felt it was important enough to tell me, I figured it must have been significant. So, as he continued to explain, I paid close attention.

"The problem when there's an injury right before a fight is scheduled to be fought is that tickets have already been sold, venues have been rented, and money's been spent. Cancelling the fight as a whole would cost millions."

"Makes sense," I said.

"Theresa Shunk sprained her ankle last week. The official statement will come from her camp tomorrow. She can't do anything for eight weeks, so she can't fight Shay Simpson next month. The problem? No one will fight Simpson on such short notice. There's only three weeks to prepare, and fighters who had hoped to fight her in the future aren't going to embarrass themselves by stepping in and being beat when they feel if they had time to train that they'd actually win. But the money's been spent. The venue? The MGM Grand in Las Vegas. Already rented. The tickets? Sold out. Pay-per-view has taken in millions. Shay Simpson's camp needs someone to fight her, and that *someone* needs to have a record that tells the fans that it will be a great fight."

He rested his arms on the edge of his desk and leaned forward. He locked eyes with me. "That someone, Jaz, is *you*."

Shane Dekkar went from being a cool kid to being crazy in an instant. There was no way Shockwave Simpson's management team would agree to have her fight some no-name girl from Omaha, Nebraska who moved to Texas to get away from her abusive father.

"There's no way they'd agree to let me fight her. I mean, it's cool to think about and everything, but…"

"They're waiting on a call back," he said.

I sprung up from Ethan's lap. "Who's waiting?"

"Simpson's camp."

"Waiting for a call from who?"

"From Kelsey."

"About what?"

He laughed. "About you."

My throat tightened. I began to pace the floor. "You told them about me?"

He nodded. "I asked Kelsey to. And he did."

I looked at Kelsey. He stared back at me stone-faced.

I looked at Dekk. He grinned.

I swallowed hard. "What'd they say? I mean. What'd you tell them? You just. You actually called them? Like 'hey Shockwave, how's it going?' I mean you…What did you…you actually called them?"

He raised his hands, turned his palms to face me, and took a deep breath. "Here's what happened. Kelsey's my trainer and my manager. We found out about your record. He called *Tactical Promotions*, who promotes my fights, and almost every other professional fighter's fights. He gave them your stats and said you were fighting out of this gym. He told them you were going pro. He asked for them to find you a good fight for your first fight, considering your undefeated record as an amateur. In ten minutes, they called back with the news of Theresa Shunk's injury. They said to expect a call from Simpson's camp. Are you with me so far?"

I nodded. It did make sense, but there was no way that Simpson's camp would ever call back and agree to anything with *me*, I knew that much.

"We've since had that call. Actually, quite a few of them. That's why you're here. Simpson wants to fight you, Jaz. In three weeks. Would you like to hear their offer?"

I stopped pacing the floor and stared.

"Twenty-three days," Kelsey said flatly.

I turned toward Ethan. He was smiling from ear to ear.

"Offer for what?" I asked.

"Tactical Promotion's offer to have you fight."

"They'd actually pay me?"

Everyone laughed. Everyone except me.

"Yes. They'll pay you. Comparatively speaking, I don't think it's quite up to standards, but it's open for negotiation. It's unheard of to be offered a flat fee in a title fight, but that's what they're offering."

I exchanged glances between Ripp, Ethan, and Dekk. "Title fight? She's putting up the title?"

He nodded. "Kelsey required it."

My heart went nuts. A grapefruit sized lump rose in my throat. "Hold on," I said. "I need to talk to *my* managers."

Ethan was still sitting in the chair. I rested my hands on his knees and gave him a kiss. "I want to do this. It's crazy. But I want it. What do you think?"

"I want you to do it," he said. "I'm behind you one hundred percent."

I turned to face Ripp. He had been surprisingly quiet. As I made eye contact with him, I realized why. He appeared to be as excited as I was, but was waiting for my response. His right knee bounced up and down as he waited for my answer.

"You with me on this one, Boss?" I asked. "It'll be a bitch to train for."

His nodded his head eagerly. "If you agree, I agree. But on one condition."

"What's that?"

"It's me and Kelsey, together. We're in it to win it," he said.

The thought of having the old man at my side made me happy. "Okay."

I turned around. "I'll do it."

"You want to hear their offer?"

"I uhhm. I don't care. I mean, I don't care what they'll pay. Call 'em back. Tell 'em yes."

"I'm gonna tell 'em to go fuck a goat," Kelsey said. "There ain't another woman on the planet that'd agree to fight Simpson in three weeks. And they damned sure can't get anyone else that's gonna keep the interest as good as someone with a 135-0 record."

"What'd they offer?" I asked.

"One point five for a loss, and two point five for a win. Flat fees. That's horseshit. Percentage of pay-per-view's what's standard. Sixty-forty split's standard. That pretentious bitch. I'd like to…" he stood from his seat and clenched his fists. "I say we tell her to get real with her offer or get someone else."

"What do you mean, point this and point that? What's that mean for me?"

Everyone had another laugh. And, once again, it was everyone except me.

"One point five million dollars, Spaz. American money," Kelsey said. "And two point five million if you beat her."

I stopped pacing the floor and stumbled toward Ethan, who was now standing. I pointed to our chair. "I need to sit down."

But I didn't.

I threw up instead.

THIRTY

JAZ

Day eighty-five.

In a successful training regimen, sleeping is believed to be as important as exercise and eating. Ethan had been staying over regularly since our talk, and having him at my side in the morning made it difficult to get out of bed.

I was convinced sleeping with Ethan had become an important part of my training.

"Isn't life interesting?" he asked.

I rolled to my side and flopped my arm over his bare chest. "What do you mean?"

"Two and a half months ago, I didn't even know you. Now? You're fighting for a title fight, and Ripp agreed to train me. I just…" He turned his head to the side and kissed me. "I can't imagine life without you."

I got lost on his blue eyes for a moment, and then began to admire his messy hair. I had grown to love how it was never combed, but was always a perfect disaster. "I can't imagine life without you, either. It's been two and a half months? Already?"

"Crazy, huh?"

I slipped my hand over his bicep and pulled him close. "Yeah."

"It'll be awesome when Ripp can start. I can't wait."

I laid my head against his chest. "I'm sorry it won't be until after my fight."

His hands slid along my bare back and came to rest at my waist. "Right now, training you is more important. I've been this long with my trainer, a few more weeks won't hurt anything."

"Your next fight's when, next week?"

"Yeah, four days. Hopefully my last with Brockman."

The sound of his voice resonated through his chest and against my ear. There wasn't anything especially sensual about it, but for whatever reason, I found *feeling* the sound of his voice as he spoke to be a turn-on.

I pressed my ear firmly to his chest. "Say something else."

"What?"

"Anything."

"I want you to meet my parents."

I craned my neck, but kept my ear flat to his chest. "Really?"

"Uh huh. I think it's overdue. Are you okay with that?"

I liked the thought of meeting them. It was yet another step in the right direction as far as our relationship was concerned. Further proof that Ethan was in my life for a reason.

"I'd like that."

I laid still for a moment and listened to his heartbeat. I found it to be comforting, and the predictable pattern soon lulled me into a state of conscious slumber. I remained there for some time, thinking about having in-laws being a permanent part of my life.

I worried for a fleeting moment how they might accept me, and then decided that I had nothing to be ashamed of. "Do you think they'll like me?"

"I know they'll like you."

I grinned at the thought. "I love you."

I reached between his legs and began to stroke him slowly and softly. "I love you, too."

Within a few strokes, he was firm in my hand. Without speaking, I tossed my leg over his waist, situated myself, and guided him into my wetness.

Seeing his handsome face and feeling his girth inside if me at the same time was too much. I closed my eyes.

Giving Ethan my heart allowed me to exhale, which was something I had waited a lifetime to do. Immediately, I began to feel an entirely different level of satisfaction when we were together. Now, seated deep inside of me, an entire host of new feelings sat poised and ready to be released.

With each stroke of his cock, a few of them managed to escape.

They fluttered about inside of me. I buried my fingernails into his muscular chest, arched my back, and opened my eyes.

I looked down. He gazed back at me, his eyes filled with love.

Seeing his level of satisfaction caused a few of them to free themselves, riding on the backs of my pleasure filled moans.

Methodically, I worked my hips back and forth, taking time to make certain I used each and every inch of his length to my satisfaction. His massive girth stretched me to my limit each time we made love, and it was that combination of pleasure and pain that satisfied the sexual beast within me.

I gripped his massive chest firmly, digging the tips of my fingers against the flesh. In turn, he dragged his fingers along my back and bucked his hips in perfect time with the movement of my hips.

His upward thrusts buried the tip of his cock deep within me, each time forcing the breath from my lungs like a shot.

I chewed against my lower lip and closed my eyes, allowing myself to focus on the feeling of having him inside of me. Together, we continued to our quest for sexual satisfaction, grinding against each other wildly.

His girth increased. His breathing became irregular and heavy. Knowing he was on the verge of reaching climax caused me to quickly rise to my own peak of sensual satisfaction.

A tingling from within me gave warning of what was to come. I opened my eyes. He looked back at me and thrust his hips, filling me with his entire length.

I gasped out in pleasure, and with the last thrust of our successive hips, we reached climax together.

In love.

And as one.

THIRTY-ONE

JAZ

Day eighty-nine.

It was the night of Ethan's fight, and once again, he predicted a win. In fact, he said he never wanted to lose another fight, and promised to fight each and every fight to the best of his ability. Somehow, it seemed he had found a way to live a humble life and be victorious at the same time.

Personally, I felt that it was me that brought on the humility, but then again, that was just my thought on the matter. He believed it was in anticipation of having Ripp train him, but that was only a guess.

Either way, I was pleased.

"Are you excited?"

"About what?" Ripp asked.

"The fight?"

He tilted his head toward me. "Yours?" He then shifted his eyes toward Ethan. "Or his?"

I squeezed Ethan's hand. "His."

"Kind of." He chuckled. "Yours? I've been sick since we made the announcement. Got the fuckin' bubbleguts. Probably end up shittin' my pants right there in Vegas on national television."

"I doubt that."

"Are you really nervous?" Ethan asked.

"Are you fuckin' kiddin'? I'm as nervous as a nun at a penguin shoot."

Ethan and I laughed and Ripp shook his head. He claimed to be nervous, but during training, he was nothing but professional. Well, as professional as he was able to be. He was still funny and although he was big and gruff, he was always caring.

Always.

"What do you got? Forty-five minutes?" Ripp asked.

Ethan looked at his watch. "Yeah. Roughly."

"Where's your trainer?"

Ethan shrugged. "Don't know. But we're generally not here this early."

"That's no shit. What? You two stop fuckin' on fight nights?"

"Oh hell no," I said. "We boned before we left."

Ripp scowled at me and then turned toward Ethan. "Seriously?"

Ethan shrugged. "Uh huh."

"I fuckin' swear," Ripp complained. "Nobody's willin' to commit when it comes to this sport. Not like back in the day."

I laughed. "Back in the day?"

"Back in the day I used to fuck me three or four bitches a day. I'd bang 'em in the parking lot at the grocery store, behind the Japanese joint, in my car, on my bike, shit...I even beat dude's asses and fucked their ol' ladies. But one thing I never did? Fuck on fight day."

I had my doubts that he was totally truthful.

"I call bullshit."

"Call whatever you want," Ripp growled. "It's the fuckin' truth. Now Dekk? Different story right there. He'd fuck Kace and step in the ring."

"And he's undefeated, right?" I cocked an eyebrow. "And you're not."

"Fuck off, Jaz."

"Shit," Ethan said, the tone of his voice seeming almost concerned.

I leaned forward and shot him a look. "What?"

"Here he comes."

"He, who?"

"Tiny. The guy I'm fighting."

I coughed a laugh. "He goes by *Tiny*?"

He tossed his head toward the entrance.

Ripp and I both turned toward the door. Wearing a wife beater, sweats, and flip-flops, a man with a six-inch tall Mohawk haircut was walking down the aisle toward us. From what I could see, he was every bit as big as Ripp, and Ripp was beyond compare.

I fought to swallow. "You're fighting *him*?"

He crossed his arms in front of his chest and nodded. I took another glance in Tiny's direction. Surprised at the speed of his pace, I quickly turned back toward Ethan.

Out of my peripheral, I watched him. He began to chuckle. I took another quick glance. He stepped within a few feet of me and pulled his gym bag strap over his shoulder. Then, he crossed his arms, mimicked Ethan's stance, and looked right at me.

"Keep turning around and lookin', and you might convince me to give you some of this." He thrust his hips back and forth wildly in my direction.

Fucking asshole.

I clenched my right fist and threw a right hook into his chin. The sound of bone hitting bone followed and his eyes went wide.

And then, everything happened at the same time.

He rubbed his jaw and dropped his bag. "You fucking bitch."

"Motherfucker!" Ripp shouted. He yanked me to the side by my shirt. "I'm gonna fuckin' kill you!"

"Come on, big boy," Tiny bellowed. He curled his clenched fists toward his chest.

Oh fuck.

Ripp took a fighting stance.

Above all of the shouting, Ethan screamed. His tone and the authority in his voice sent a chill down my spine. Oddly, it also provided me a strange sense of well-being.

"Don't fucking touch him!" Ethan growled. "Don't. Fucking. Touch. Him."

He wasn't angry. Or even mad. He was ready to kill.

"I got this," Ripp said over his shoulder.

"I meant what I said, Ripp," Ethan said, his voice demanding. "I'll defend what's mine, and I don't need any fucking help."

Tiny kicked off his flip-flops. "Come on, pretty boy. When I'm done with ya, I'll butt fuck ya, and then I'll get started on your girl."

Ethan stepped around Ripp. As soon as he did, Tiny swung a right hook. Ethan dodged it, and immediately swung a hard right hand into the side of Tiny's face.

Tiny stumbled.

Ethan hit him again with another right.

And again.

And again.

Tiny stumbled away from the ring and into the aisle leading to the gym's exit. People began to gather around.

As Tiny fought to regain his footing, he swung a hopeful left. Ethan leaned back and the punch swung past him. He countered with a straight left, and it landed dead center on Tiny's nose.

Blood splattered everywhere.

And Tiny fell onto the concrete floor.

"Motherfucker," Ethan said. "Get up."

Tiny moaned.

Ethan shoved the heel of his boot against Tiny's ribs. "I said get up."

There was no way he could get up. Ethan had hit him with five unanswered punches, all of which landed and landed hard. If anything, he needed an ambulance.

Ethan leaned over him and grabbed a fistful of his Mohawk. Using his hair and the back of his sweats, he hoisted him onto his feet. His once white shirt was covered in blood, as was his face.

"Apologize," Ethan said. "Tell her you're sorry for how you acted, cocksucker."

Tiny moaned.

Ethan grabbed him by the throat and squeezed. "Apologize."

"Don't kill him," Ripp said.

"He's going to apologize," Ethan growled.

"Sorry," Tiny said, his voice and almost inaudible whisper.

"Not good enough," Ethan said.

He released his throat. "Apologize."

Tiny shook his head and coughed a few times. Blood steadily trickled down his face. He looked like absolute hell. "I...uhhm. I'm...I'm sorry."

Ethan met my gaze. "Satisfied?"

I nodded. "Very much so."

Ethan wrapped his arm around Tiny's neck, picked up his gym bag,

199

and dragged him all the way to the door. After kicking the door open with his foot, he shoved him and his bag out into the parking lot.

Ripp looked at my hand. "Did you hurt your knuckles?"

I shook my hand. Although it was sore, nothing was broken. Contrary to what is shown in movies and on television, beating someone with bare fists generally either displaces or breaks fingers. Mine, however was just sore. "It'll be fine."

"Now that was an ass whippin'," Ripp said as Ethan walked up.

Ethan looked at his bloody hands. "He got what he deserved."

Ripp chuckled. "God damned sure did."

"Might need to take some time off fighting." Ethan held his hands up. All of his knuckles were mangled terribly.

"You're gonna need some stitches," Ripp said. "Or we can glue 'em."

Ethan laughed. "I'll get them stitched. And not by you."

He turned toward me. "Sorry about that."

"About what?"

"How he treated you."

"It's not your fault," I said. "And you took care of it. Good thing, I was gonna whip his Mohawk wearing ass."

"You better take care of those hands," Ripp said.

Terrance, the kid who cleaned the gym, pushed a mop and a bucket between us. "Clean up on aisle seven."

We all shared a laugh as he mopped up the blood.

After he finished, he plopped the mop into the bucket and leaned against the handle. "What was that about?"

"About a man who doesn't know how to be respectful to a lady," Ripp said.

Ethan nodded. "What he said."

"If I was disrespectful to a lady, I'd be slapped so hard my grandkids will feel it. That's what my pop tells me."

"Your pop sounds like a good man," Ripp said.

Terrance grinned and nodded his head. "Alright, then. Try and stay out of trouble."

After a few minutes of talking, we agreed Ethan needed to go to the minor emergency center for stitches.

"I'm gonna go talk to Dekk," Ripp said.

"I'm driving him to the doctor," I said.

"Tomorrow," Ripp said over his shoulder.

Ethan and I walked to the door and I jokingly pushed it open for him. "Don't want you any more banged up than you already are."

He stepped through the door, turned toward me, and chuckled. "I'm fine. Ten or twelve stitches and…"

Out of nowhere, something hit him in the head. It came so fast it took me a minute to realize what had happened, but by the time my mind processed it, it was too late.

He fell flat onto the asphalt.

I rushed through the door. Tiny stood over him with crazy eyes and a baseball bat. Unconscious, Ethan lay on his back with his hands at his sides.

Oh my God.

Tiny raised the bat over his head.

"No!" I yelled. "Don't!"

He glanced at me, grinned, and swung the bat down hard, crashing it into Ethan's skull.

I couldn't believe what I was seeing.

"Nooooo!" I cried.

I fell to my knees and thrust myself over Ethan, protecting his body with mine. I raised my right arm in defense. "Please. Please," I blubbered. "Don't. You're going to kill him."

I looked down. Ethan's skull was split open. Blood was everywhere. I cradled his head in my hands. Someone came through the door and screamed.

"Get Ripp," I cried out. "And call 911. We need an ambulance. Hurry!"

I reached into his bag, pulled out his sleeveless sweatshirt, and wrapped it around his bloody skull.

And I cried like I had never cried before.

THIRTY-TWO

JAZ

Day ninety.

It wasn't the way I wanted to meet Ethan's parents, but I had very little choice. Dekk, Ripp, Kelsey, Ethan's mother and father, his siblings, and a doctor were all in the waiting room.

"There are so many factors, Mr. Halloway. The damage to the skull was severe, therefore the damage to the brain was severe. There are issues with secondary damage due to inadequate cerebral oxygenation, and we have no way of knowing the effects on a grand scale. It's simply too early to tell."

"When will he be awake?" his father asked.

His mother moved her hand away from her mouth. "He doesn't know, William."

"He knows. He's the doctor," he growled. He turned away from Ethan's mother and faced the doctor again. "When?"

"I'm sorry," the doctor said. "Right now, it's not a matter of when. I don't want to mislead you. It's a matter of *if*. And an awfully big if."

Oh God.

Ripp hugged me.

The police had already arrested Tiny. It came as no shock to me that he had several warrants for his arrest. Personally, I wished the police hadn't found him. Street justice, in my opinion, is best in some circumstances.

This was one of them.

I attempted to prepare myself for the worst, but couldn't. Each time I tried to imagine Ethan dying, it caused me to start blubbering uncontrollably.

Fighting didn't matter. Championships didn't matter. Money didn't matter. Nothing mattered but having Ethan healthy and back in my arms.

"Want to go get a coffee?" Ripp asked.

"You hate coffee," I said. "Ethan…"

I started to say *Ethan told me*, but couldn't even say his name. I bit into my lip, reached for Ripp's hand, and nodded. Grateful that I had him not only as my trainer, but as a friend, I followed him as he turned toward the hallway.

It seemed that there were three groups of people concerned with Ethan's recovery. All of his friends, his siblings, and then his parents. They had no interest in mingling with us, talking to us, or sharing information. What little we had learned was from overhearing what the doctor said while speaking to his parents.

Oddly, Ethan's brother and sister were seated in another area of the waiting room altogether, on a couch. They seemed to have no interest in Ethan's parents, us, or the doctor.

I wanted it all to end, and everything to go back to normal.

Ripp stomped down the hallway with my hand in his. I fought to catch up to him and recalled the first day of training when he all but dragged me into the sporting goods store. "Slow down."

"Sorry, Jaz," he said. "I'm just mad I didn't kill that motherfucker myself."

"That's all you need to do. Kill someone else," Dekk said. "Justice will be served. The security cameras got it all. That guy's fucked."

"You uhhm. You…killed someone."

Ripp stopped. "I ain't proud of it, but yeah. This fucktard did my sister real bad. Raped her. I went to his house, we got into it, and I broke his fuckin' neck."

"Did you go to prison?"

"Self-defense," he said. "He pulled a gun."

"Oh," I said. "I'm sorry about your sister."

He shrugged "Happily married now."

It surprised me, but it didn't. Ripp seemed like the kind of guy that would do anything to protect the people he loved. To think of his sister being raped was awful. Realizing Ripp took care of the situation, and of the person who did it, however, was oddly satisfying.

The four of us went to the cafeteria, bought drinks, and sat down. For some time, no one spoke.

"The kid's got a huge heart. That'll get him through a lot," Kelsey said, breaking the silence. "Damned good how he stood up for you. Show's how much you mean to him. Now, it's your turn. You're a strong woman, Spaz. Stay strong. We'll all get through this together."

I liked that Kelsey called me Spaz even when things were serious. It let me know the nickname he'd given me was more out of affection than out of spite.

"I'll be strong," I said. "I don't have a choice."

"None of us do," Ripp said. "Every damned one of us is a fighter. It's in our blood. Ethan included. We need to fight out here, and be strong for him. He'll fight his own fight down the hall in ICU. I look at it this way: he's sleepin' right now. That fuck bubble hurt him real bad, and he just needs to sleep it off. Hell, as tough as he is, he probably ain't hurt that bad."

I thought of Ethan's skull, and how it was split open when the ambulance arrived. My stomach convulsed. I reached across the table. Rip extended his arm and grabbed my hand.

I squeezed it in mine, once again grateful that I had him as a friend. While I stared blankly off in the distance, I felt someone's fingers against my other hand. I looked down. Kelsey had my hand in his, cupping it lightly.

I gripped his hand in return.

I glanced at Dekk.

He didn't speak, but simply gave me a nod of his head, grinned his shallow grin, and pulled his hood over his head.

And I knew I was where I needed to be.

With the only family I had.

But it was all the family I needed.

THIRTY-THREE

JAZ

Day ninety-three.

Juggling work, training, and my visits to the hospital wasn't easy. At least twice a day I made it to see Ethan, then worked and trained for the fight as I was able.

I knew all three things were important, but in different ways. Upon waking up, if Ethan found out I'd given up on my title fight, he'd be pretty disappointed with me. That reason alone motivated me to continue training. I had to work to pay my rent and eat, so it was a necessity as well.

Seeing Ethan, even as he slept his days away in a coma, remained the highlight of my day.

The skin under his eyes was bruised terribly, as were his cheeks, and all of his pretty hair was gone. It wasn't anything a hat couldn't fix, so I bought him a stocking cap. I tried to find the good in it all, and thanked God that the man responsible for harming him was in custody. I also thanked God that Ethan was alive during every visit and every night before bed. In my prayers I explained that I'd settle for him the way he was if it was all I could get.

Either way, I loved Ethan with all my heart, and I knew nothing could change the way I felt.

I rode the elevator up to the seventh floor and came around the corner toward the nurse's station. Technically, I wasn't even supposed to be in Ethan's room, because I wasn't family. Dekk took care of that with a few phone calls, and once again I was grateful for my makeshift family.

"Good morning, Jaz," the nurse said.

"Hi, Tracey."

I walked down the hallway and stepped through the open door leading into Ethan's intensive care room. The constant beeping provided reassurance that he was alive and well. I leaned over the bed and kissed his cheek.

"Good morning, Babe."

I sat down in the chair, opened the crossword puzzle book, and started the day's puzzle.

"Ready? Four letters. *Broadway dud*. That's down. And across? Three letters. *Mr. Franklin.*"

I lifted the pen to the page. "Let's go with *Ben* for Mr. Franklin. So, four letters down, Broadway dud, and starts with a 'B'. We'll go with *bomb*. Okay. At the end of Bomb, we've got a good one. The clue is *implore*. So, what starts with a 'B' and has seven letters?"

"Beseech?" I reached over and patted his leg. "Good answer."

"How's the crossword comin'?" Kelsey asked as he walked through the door.

"Good, thank you."

He patted me on the shoulder. "What time you working today?"

"In about fifty minutes. At nine. I got a morning shift, and I'll go until after dinner, but I don't have to close."

"That's good."

I studied him for a moment. "Are you wearing the same clothes you were wearing yesterday?"

"I always wear a white tee shirt."

"But your white tee shirt doesn't always have ketchup on the sleeve."

He looked at the sleeve, shrugged, and sat down. "Haven't been home yet."

"You stayed all night?"

"Right where you're sittin'. Somebody's got to be here if he wakes up. Can't decide if his folks are too busy or don't care. Don't matter much, I suppose, as long as someone's here."

I felt terrible for Kelsey. He loved each and every one of us, but he wasn't about to admit it. Seeing how much time and effort he put into making sure Ethan had everything he needed was proof of his love for us all.

On the second day, Kelsey went to the store and bought socks, claiming that the socks they'd provided were too tight and might cut off circulation. Later in the day he went to the CVS store and bought lotion, stating that Ethan's skin was drying out from the *dime store bullshit* the hospital provided.

When he learned of my idea to read the crossword puzzles, he provided all the reassurance I needed to convince me it would keep Ethan alert and not allow his brain to fade away to nothing.

"Thank you for caring," I said.

"So we're passing out thanks today for bein' human? Well thank you, too, Spaz," he grunted.

"You know what I mean."

He shook his head. "Don't guess I do. I'm just a bored old man. What else am I gonna do?"

"When you're at the gym, you always stomp off and say 'I've got shit to do.' So, what? Now you're bored?"

"That's what I said."

I folded the crossword puzzle and glared at him.

He glared back.

After a lengthy glare-off, I gave up. "You win."

"At what? Tryin' to get a teeny bopper to mind her own business?"

"I'm not a teeny bopper. I'm twenty-five. You know it, you were at my birthday."

"I've got boots older than you," he said.

"I'm sure you do."

"If he's still here during the fight, we need to make sure they've got it playin' in here. Remind me to ask the nurse about pay-per-view. Can't have him in here without being able to hear it."

"I'll remind you. But I think he'll be fine by then."

"Just in case," he said.

I hadn't really thought about it, but at some point I was going to have to leave Ethan to go to Vegas for the fight. In fact, we'd all be gone. I thought about if for a moment, and decided I didn't like thinking about it at all, so I stopped.

I glanced up. Kelsey was fast asleep in the chair. I looked at my watch. It was past time for me to leave, so I stood and walked toward the door. I hesitated at the threshold and turned around.

"Kelsey," I whispered.

"Kelsey."

He didn't budge.

Good.

I tip-toed up behind him, bent over, and kissed him on the head.

We love you, old man.

THIRTY-FOUR

JAZ

Day ninety-nine.

Ethan had been asleep for a little more than a week without making any measurable progress. I learned that the entire thing was nothing but a glorified waiting game, and that when it came right down to it, the doctors knew absolutely nothing useful.

There were no additional tests. No one prodded his brain with a probe, nor did they place him back into the MRI machine. Neither a doctor or a nurse came to stretch his fingers and toes to make sure they still moved. They didn't work his legs back and forth.

And they only bathed him once a week.

I hated that he had to be there, and wished I could take him home with me, but I couldn't. They didn't actually *care* about him, and realizing it bothered me.

"We've got six days," Ripp said. "Six."

"I know."

"Do you think you're ready?"

"As ready as I'm going to get. I'm not going to learn anything in six days, am I?"

He shrugged. "Suppose not."

"I'm not going to be bigger, stronger, or faster, am I?"

"Doubt it."

"So, I think I'm ready."

"I wish things were different with him. You know that, right?"

"I know."

"Tell you the truth, I wish I would have kicked the fuckers ass like I was goin' to," he said. "If I would have beat his ass, Ethan would be right here, right now. He wouldn't be in that fuckin' hospital, that's for sure."

"It's not your fault."

"I didn't do it, but I could have prevented it. Next time? I'll do what I know is right."

"Ethan was defending my honor. Is that wrong?"

He shook his head. "No. But I was doing the same thing."

"You and me? We're not together. So you were just…I don't know. Just--"

"It's a man's responsibility to stand up for any woman who is being mistreated, no matter who she is."

"You really think so?"

He shook his head. "Know so."

With his forehead wrinkled and his eyes narrow, he looked angry. I suppose deep down inside, he felt no differently than I did. Thinking that there were two people who felt like me didn't make me feel any better. I wouldn't wish my feelings on anyone.

I was exhausted mentally, physically, and emotionally. I walked over to him and held out my gloves. He untied them, pulled them off, and tossed them on top of my bag.

I wrapped my arms around him and gave him a hug. "I'm sorry you're angry about all this. One of these days he'll be fine, and we'll all look back on it and…well…I don't know. Maybe we'll tell stories or something."

"Something," he said. "We'll do something."

"It's the weekend. Can we quit so I can go up there?"

He held me close for a long minute, then pushed his hands against my shoulders, causing me to lean away from him a little bit.

He gazed down at me. "You go take care of *him*," he said. "When it comes to this fight? I'll take care of you. You're ready, Jaz. As ready as you're gonna get."

"Thank you. I just. I don't know. I want to go give him a bath. Clean him up a little bit."

"Do whatever you've got to do," he said.

I thought about it for what seemed like forever, then decided to just ask. "Can I tell you *anything*?"

He nodded. "Anything."

"Anything?"

"What'd I just say? You can tell me anything," he said.

I really needed to hear it from someone. I was afraid if I didn't I was just going to collapse and die. I prayed he would understand. I inhaled a shallow breath and sighed.

"I love you, Ripp."

He grinned the cheesy Mike Ripton grin. "Shit. I love you, too, you little fucker."

It wasn't what I had in mind, but there was no doubt in my mind that it was heartfelt.

I reached for my bag. "Okay. I'm going to go see him, and then get some sleep."

"Tell him I said 'hi'," he said. "After you're done with the bath, though."

I shouldered my bag and stared back at him. "Why not during?"

"Don't want you washin' his pecker while you're talking to him about me. Might confuse him."

I rolled my eyes and turned away. Ripp didn't have much tact, and he lacked conventional manners, but I wouldn't trade him for anything or anyone.

***

I glared at him. "Where's Kelsey?"

Ethan's father tossed his hands in the air. "I have no idea who Kelsey is, and to be honest, I don't care."

"Kelsey is the one who has been up here all day and night sitting with him in case he wakes up. And I don't think you get to make those decisions."

"If I don't, who will?"

Tears rolled down my cheeks. "You're not God," I blubbered.

"Right now I'm the closest thing to God that exists," he said.

I wiped my cheeks on my forearm. "If you love him, you'd never even talk about doing anything like that."

"Who do you suppose will be stuck with the bill? When he doesn't wake up? Not you, that's for certain."

I was beyond tears. I had reached a point I was angry enough to fight, but felt I owed it to Ethan to be as civil as I was capable of. "I'll pay it. Here in a week, I'll be able to. So just leave. Just go. I'll pay it."

"Highly unlikely," he said. "And I'm not going to argue with you. I don't owe you an explanation."

I felt worse than sick thinking that he was even considering it. I had no idea people like him even existed. "It's been nine days. Nine. Not nine years. Not even nine months. And I don't care how long it is, I'll be here with him forever. You know why?"

"I don't care."

"Because I love him," I shouted.

"Is there a problem?" Kelsey asked from behind me.

Thank God.

I spun around and hugged him. After sobbing into the shoulder of his shirt for several seconds, I gathered my composure. I leaned back and wiped my tears. "He's going to have them unplug Ethan. He wants to let him die."

"He's brain dead," Ethan's father said. "Someone has to make decisions about what's in everyone's best interest."

Kelsey stepped around me. "He ain't brain dead, he's recovering from an injury." He doubled up his fists and puffed out his chest. "Now get your shit and get out of here before I drag your ass out."

Holy crap, Kelsey.

Ethan's father glared back at him. "And you are?"

"I'm the old man you don't want to fuck with right now. Believe me."

"It's a matter of economics."

Kelsey stepped aside and pointed toward the door. "Economics? This is about money? You can bet your bottom god forsaken dollar that I've got a lot more god damned money than you do. I'll spend every last cent keepin' this kid alive and paying attorneys to make sure you don't have a say in matters. Now, get out of here before I bust your fuckin' nose."

Ethan's father shook his head. "Sooner or later--"

Kelsey raised his fists as if he was actually prepared to fight. "Sooner or later? Sooner or later I'm gonna whip your ass. Leave. Now."

Ethan's father stomped out.

I exhaled, feeling like I had inherited an entirely new set of problems. "We can't leave him alone. His dad will--"

Kelsey shook his head and sat down. "He won't be alone."

"But--"

"But nothing. He won't be alone."

"I love him so much," I said.

My eyes welled with tears. The crying started all over again. "I can't let anything happen…"

"Nothing's gonna happen to this kid," Kelsey said. "Not on my watch."

He clenched his fist and extended his arm.

What little doubt that remained vanished.

And I pounded my fist into his.

THIRTY-FIVE

JAZ

Day one hundred three.

I felt sick about leaving to go to Las Vegas, but I knew I had no alternative. "You promise you'll call if anything changes?"

Kelsey glared at me. "What'd I tell ya?"

"Anything. I mean it."

"I know what *anything* means."

I hated thinking about Kelsey not being at the fight. "I wish you could go. But, I'm glad not you're going. You know what I mean. Staying here to be with him."

He rolled his eyes dramatically. "Listen to the dummy, Spaz. And keep twisting on the ball of that foot like your putting out a cigarette. You'll do fine."

"I will," I said. "Just like you told me."

I glanced at my watch. "I've got to go."

He nodded.

I stepped to the edge of the bed, reached up, and adjusted his stocking cap. "It's a hundred one outside, and it's so cold in here, you're going to end up sick. I'll talk to them about the temperature again, don't worry. I've got to go, but I'll be back in a few days, so don't worry. No promises, but win or lose, I'll make you proud."

I leaned over and gave him a kiss. "I love you."

I glanced at my watch. "Shit. I've really got to--"

Kelsey opened his arms. "Come here."

I mashed my face into his chest, wrapped my arms around him, and held him tight. He might have been a grumpy old fucker, but he was the most awesome grumpy old fucker to ever exist.

He hugged me for a moment, and then released me. "Get out of here."

"If anything changes," I said.

"Heard you the first ten times."

I sighed and turned away.

I was almost to the corridor, and I heard him shout. "Hey Spaz!"

I turned around.

"I love ya," he said.

It felt good to hear him say it. I started to respond, and then paused. He stood in the center of the hallway staring back at me. I grinned and turned toward the exit.

And, after a few steps, I raised my right hand high in the air and flipped him the bird.

THIRTY-SIX

JAZ

Day one hundred five.

I stood in the corner of the ring surrounded by 17,000 people. Coming down the aisle wasn't at all what I expected. There was no cheering, no one slapped my hands, and there were no legions of screaming fans.

Only Ripp and me.

"I feel funny," I whispered.

"I'm gonna shit my drawers," Ripp whispered. "And watch what you say. They've got them zoom in cameras and microphones everywhere."

I nodded. "Okay."

Shockwave came down the aisle. The entire crowd went ballistic. One day, if I continued to be a contender, I would have a following no different than she did. But my followers? Mine would be different. I wouldn't talk shit to everyone and send out hashtag shit talk tweets on Twitter, so my fans would be classy.

But I'd be a bitch in the ring.

She ducked under the ropes, stepped inside the ring, and glared at me.

I pursed my lips, glared back, and waited.

"Don't forget what I told ya," Ripp said. "Touch 'em up when the ref tells you to, and after that, no matter how many times she offers, don't pound gloves with her."

"Got it."

I liked Ripp's thought process on touching gloves. He said after the initial 'shake', to never touch gloves again when offered. It was an intimidation tactic he said he used, and he swore it worked.

According to him, it made his opponent fear him.

I needed all the help I could get.

The announcer reached for the microphone. "Ladies and gentlemen…"

"Tonight, Tactical Promotions and the MGM Grand present the WBC championship bout scheduled for ten rounds."

"The challenger, in the blue corner, with a career record of 135 wins and 0 losses, with 62 wins by knockout. In her professional debut, Jaz… Brawler…Briscoe!"

I raised my gloves and turned in a circle.

A handful of people, Dekk included, cheered.

I felt small. Microscopic, to be honest. But I wasn't intimidated. Not at all.

"And, in the red corner, the champion…"

The crowd went wild. As they screamed and cheered, he continued. "With a professional record of…"

"I hate this girl," I whispered. "Hashtag Shockwave. Seriously? Hashtags are stupid."

"You ain't the only one. She's so fuckin' full of herself…"

"Shay…Shockwave…Simpson…"

The crowd went wild.

Again.

The referee called us to the center. Ripp and I went together. She stood with her trainer and manager. She glared at me. I glared back.

"I gave you your instructions in the dressing rooms. Obey my commands at all times. When I say break, I want a clean break. In the event of a knock down, I'll direct you to a neutral corner. I want a clean fight. No low blow, and I *will* call them. Understood?"

He looked at her. She nodded.

He looked at me.

"Yes, Sir."

"Protect yourselves at all times. Any questions?"

He looked at her. She shook her head.

He looked at me.

"No, Sir"

"Touch 'em up."

I pounded my gloves into hers and turned away.

Ripp patted his hand against my shoulder. "You ready?"

I pounded my gloves together. "Hashtag fuck yes."

THIRTY-SEVEN

JAZ

Day one hundred five.

Her intensity was undeniable. From the instant she was within reach, she began to pummel me with two and three punch combinations, leaving me very little choice but to protect myself from being beaten to death.

We knew she was a versatile fighter. She wasn't champion by accident, that was for sure. She'd been on top for four years, and since becoming champion, she hadn't been beaten. Having an undefeated record in the amateurs is one thing. Being undefeated in the professional circuit is a completely different animal.

Dekk and Ripp agreed if I could get through a round with her and figure out what her strengths and weaknesses were, the rest of the fight would be able to be fought knowing exactly how to attack her.

Taking the fight to her was my strength, and to date, no one had really done so. Almost every opponent she had fought was forced to fight a defensive fight against her. Being stuck on the receiving end of her punch parade wasn't on my list of to-do's, though.

Her barrage of punches stopped. I peered through the space between my gloves and saw an opening.

They said not to attack you in the first round, but I need to know if you can take a punch.

I feigned a right and swung a left hook. The left crashed into her ribcage and caused her to lean to her right as she winced in pain.

Hit hard for a little bitch, don't I?

As she leaned to her right, exposing her left side to me, I swung a right hook as hard as I could.

At that instant, pissing off Dekk or Ripp wasn't my concern. I wanted to let her know that she wasn't in for a free ride. My hand came down hard against her jaw, sending her stumbling toward the ropes.

I rushed toward her, pounding her with shots to the body. One after another, I punched and pushed until she was against the ropes. My attack had only been for a few seconds, but it was a few seconds of absolute hell for her.

My only focus was keeping her against the ropes. There was no hospital, no trainer, no grumpy old men, and no bills to pay. There was a girl against the ropes, and I needed to keep her there for as long as I could.

With my gloves raised just beneath my chin and my elbows tucked to my sides, I shoved my forearms against her, pushing her into the ropes. As she sprung back toward me, I swung an uppercut.

It connected pretty nicely against her chin. She reacted with a straight left that I easily dodged.

I've seen enough.

I stepped away from her and moved to the center of the ring. I chose to do it as more of an insult to her than anything. To have her pinned against the ropes and walk away would send a clear message that I was there to fight. She *should* know it. The crowd would know it, and that was my hope. I needed to get the crowd behind me.

I stood in the center of the ring and glared.

She shook her head, pounded her gloves into her stomach, and began to shuffle toward me.

Come on, bitch. Let's go.

She had her hands held high as she came toward me. Really high. Her elbows were tucked tight to her sides. It was apparent she didn't like me hitting her face and she intended on protecting it.

There was only one problem with having her gloves up so high.

It left her mid-section exposed.

I unleashed a six shot combination to her stomach and ribs with all of the power I had saved from the beginning of the round. Her gloves lowered slightly.

I swung a hard straight right and connected with her chin.

Her eyes bulged.

Her legs buckled.

I felt Ripp pound his fist against the mat twice.

I cocked my left hand.

Ding!

The bell sounded, signaling the end of the round.

Consider yourself lucky.

I was getting ready to hurt your ass, bitch.

I turned toward Ripp and began to walk confidently to my corner.

He jumped up and shot me a glare.

Sorry Boss, I just had to hit that bitch.

He reached for my mouthpiece. "What the fuck were you doing?"

"Seeing if she can take a punch."

"Huge mistake lettin' her off those fuckin' ropes. It's pretty fuckin' clear she can't fight on the ropes. Get her back on 'em and take it to her. You hear me?"

I nodded.

"I asked you a fuckin' question," he snapped back.

I swallowed hard. "Yes, Sir."

"No fucking around. No showboatin'. No bullshit. Get that bitch on the ropes and keep her there. She don't like it. Now, listen up. One more thing. Your hard right? Follow it up with the left hook. Not a jab, and damned sure not an uppercut. A hook to the head. Hard right, hook to the head. Got it?"

I nodded.

"Say it," he demanded.

"Hard right. Hook to the head. Keep her on the ropes."

It seemed like I was only resting for two or three seconds and he slipped in my mouthpiece.

Ding!

THIRTY-EIGHT

JAZ

Day one hundred five.

She came at me as soon as the bell rang, trying to get me against the ropes. I used my leg strength to keep her from pushing me around, and my quick hands to remind her I wasn't going to be an easy win.

I pushed her off, and she swung a hard right hand into my ribs.

Fuck that hurts!

A left jab followed, and a right came immediately behind it.

Every one of her punches connected. And. They. Hurt.

Angered, I swung a wild left. It glanced off her shoulder. I followed up with a right hook, and the punch glanced off her hip.

She caught me with a hard right hand to the head, knocking me goofy for a split second.

I shoved my gloves into her tits and shook my head.

Oh, you wanna fight?

I stepped toward her, leading with my left foot, shuffling my right close behind. As the gap between us closed, I pressed the ball of my right foot into the mat, lifted my heel, and plowed her in the face with a hard right hand.

The punch caused her to stumble.

You can thank Kelsey for that.

I gave her a shot to the ribs and then lit her up with a quick five punch combination. When the punches stopped, she looked back at me with wide eyes.

I didn't come to box, bitch.

I came to brawl.

She swung a left hook that connected hard with my ribs. I countered with an uppercut that fell short, and then a right to her bicep. The punch to her bicep seemed to cause her more pain than anything, which struck me as odd.

I swung a wild left and followed it up with another right. The right slammed into her bicep again.

Her face contorted in pain.

Something wrong with that arm, Shockwave?

I pounded it again.

She turned to the side.

I pounded it again.

She swung a wild right.

I hit her with a hard right. The punch caught her right in the center of the chin.

Fighting amateur bouts, boxers are required to wear headgear. The cushioned pad that surrounds the head protects the fighters from concussions, cuts, and being badly bruised from being hit.

In professional boxing, there is no such head protection worn.

By my guess, when my hard right hand blasted against her chin, she wished she had some.

She stumbled toward the ropes.

Oh shit!

I rushed toward her and began to work the body. She continued to stumble backward, still trying to recover from my hard right. A few seconds later, and we were against the ropes.

I pummeled her torso with a six shot combo, and swung a left hook into the side of her neck, barely missing her head. I followed with a right into her bicep, which caused her right hand to come down slightly.

I raised my gloves to my face, and shoved against her with my elbows while I planned the next stage of my attack.

A hard left slamming into my hip brought me out of my deep thinking. She hit hard, and I didn't like it one fucking bit.

Hard right, hook to the head. Hard right, hook to the head.

I worked her body hard and took a short step back and studied her. Her left glove was hanging low. I blasted her with a hard right, and followed with a left hook. The hook caught her on the chin, twisting her face to the side and making her weak in the knees.

I followed up with four hard body shots and then stepped back.

Come on, bitch, let's fucking brawl!

I felt a pounding on the mat. Twice. Ripp's signal to me that the round was ending.

But there was no way it was the end of the round.

I waited for her to come to me.

Again, Ripp's hand slammed against the mat twice.

What the fuck?

I stepped close to her and swung a left hook into her stomach and followed with a hard right. The right caught her square in the face.

Fuck yes.

And it was at that instant that I heard it.

"BRAAAA-LER!"

A tingling ran along my spine.

I took another step.

More people joined in. The crowd was shunting my name. *My* name. "BRAAA-LER!"

I came close to being overwhelmed with emotion. I acted unaffected and thought of what Ripp had said.

Against the ropes. Hard right, then hook to the head.

He wasn't pounding the mat because the round was ending. He was pounding the mat because I wasn't listening to him. I was trying to lure her into brawl.

I took another step toward her, absorbed the punches she threw at me, and as soon as there was a lull, hammered her with a hard right hand. The punch plowed right into her mouth. Before my glove came into contact with her skin, my left was already on its way.

Boom!

The left hook knocked her to the side, and she began to stumble hard. The ropes were the only thing keeping her on her feet.

I wished I had her in the center of the ring where I wanted her so I could knock her down.

I pounded her with another right. She fell into the ropes and swung a right hand into the air.

She was hurt and it was obvious. The last three right hands caused her some damage, and she was showing it.

"When you're working your opponent on the ropes, never let up. On the ropes, always become a boxer. It'll pay off in the end."

I straightened my stance slightly.

Alright, Mike fucking Ripton. I'll box for a few seconds and see what happens.

I hit her with a quick four shot combination to the head, followed by a hard right hand. Her eyes went glassy, but she didn't fall.

"BRAW-LER..."

I swung a left hook into her jaw. She stumbled to her right.

"BRAW-LER...BRAW-LER...BRAW-LER!"

I pounded her again. This time with a straight right. Then a left. She stumbled along the ropes. I chased after her, hammering her with lefts and rights.

The ropes were her only salvation.

And then it made sense.

If we were in the center of the ring, she could have escaped after any series of punches that I'd thrown. Ripp wanted her against the ropes so she *couldn't* escape. He wanted me to give her the beating that she needed to be given without a chance of her getting away from me.

I pushed her into the ropes and blasted her with another right. Her head flopped back and forth from the impact of the punch.

She looked like a crash test dummy.

I followed with a left hook.

And another right.

And a left.

"BRAW-LER...BRAW-LER...BRAW-LER!"

My youth. My father. Ethan's current state of being. There were many things I could have claimed as my inspiration to pound her into the ropes, but they would have been lies. Fairy tale bullshit. Something for a book about my life. Or whatever...

But they wouldn't have been the truth.

I was in that ring for one person.

Me.

I wasn't there to prove a point, or stand up for women's rights. I wasn't there for money or for fame.

I didn't want a shoe deal with Nike, or an Under Armour contract.

I wanted to win because despite all of the information to support the fact that I was a loser, I wasn't a loser.

I was a winner.

Hard right, then a left hook.

I hammered her with another right hand. She staggered. I inhaled a sharp breath, cocked my left, and swung it hard, raising my foot completely off of the mat.

The punch plowed into her jaw and lifted her from her feet. Her body came to a crashing *thud* at my feet.

I glared down at her. "Jaz Briscoe, bitch. Don't fucking forget it. Get your ass up, let's fight."

Ripp was right. Keeping her on the ropes was the right thing to do. When she got up, I had plans for her. I was going to lather, rinse, and fucking repeat.

The ref stepped between us and directed me to a neutral corner.

I gladly stepped to the corner, and waited for her to come to her feet so I could finish her arrogant ass off.

He reached for her arm and tried to help her up.

She fell again.

He lifted her by the arm, got her to her feet, and began to ask her questions.

She fell to the mat again.

She was hurt and she was hurt bad.

He looked into her eyes.

And he waved his arms over her, signaling the end of the fight.

The end of the fight?

What?

My lip began to quiver.

What just happened?

I looked around me. The ring was filling up with reporters, random people, and promoters.

It was over. It was *really* over.

I had won.

I shoved my way through the crowd. Sitting on my stool with his head in his hands, Ripp looked like a 240-pound child. I knelt down beside him and pushed my glove against his chin, lifting it slightly so I could look into his eyes.

I spit my mouthpiece out at the base of the stool. "What's wrong, Boss?"

He lifted his head. Tears were rolling down his cheeks.

"Nothin' For the first time in my life, everything's right." He reached up laughed, and wiped his tears. "*Everything.*"

A tear rolled down my cheek.

He stood up. "Congratulations. You did it."

I shook my head and stood. "We. *We* did it."

"Ladies and Gentlemen!"

The announcers voice rang out over the sound system. We turned toward the center of the ring. Cameras flashed. People crowded us. Microphones were everywhere. I felt like I was going to vomit.

"Ending at 1:41 of the second round, by knockout...presenting the new WBC Champion of the World..."

"Jaz Brawler Briscoe!"

Ripp gripped my wrist, raised my gloved hand high into the air, and let out a yell that was heard by millions of viewers on national television.

"Fuck Yes!" he bellowed. "We did it!"

Above the sound of everything, I heard someone scream my name.

And then, commotion. Someone was shoving their way through the crowd, shouting my name.

"It's Dekkar," I heard a reporter say. "Shane Dekkar."

"Jaz!"

I turned toward the voice.

"Jaz!"

"Get out of the fuckin' way," Ripp snarled, pushing someone to the side. "Give the girl some room."

Dekk stepped between us. Fighting to catch his breath, he held his phone out. His level of excitement was undeniable. "You need to get this."

"Kelsey?"

He shook his head. "It's the hospital. But it's not Kelsey."

He handed me the phone. "You need to brace yourself, Jaz."

I swallowed hard and raised the phone to my ear. But there was nothing I could have done to brace myself.

Nothing.

THIRTY-NINE

JAZ

Day one hundred five.

The elevator doors opened. I ran down the corridor as fast as I could, my legs burning the entire way. Ripp and Dekk were somewhere behind me, I had no idea where. Hell, I didn't care.

I slid around the corner, ran past the nurse's station, and rushed down the hallway until I was in front of the room.

724.

I took a deep breath and faced the open room.

Kelsey turned to face me.

Tears rolled down his cheeks.

He opened his mouth.

Nothing.

My lip began to quiver. I took a few slow steps. My legs began to shake. I reached for Kelsey, pulled him into me and stepped beside the bed.

"How's it...how's it...uhhm...how's it going?"

Incapable of speaking, he simply nodded.

A pen and paper sat beside the bed. I picked up the pen and scribbled a quick note.

Ethan,

235

I love you so much.
Signed,
The WBC Champion of the World

I kind of cried and kind of laughed as I placed the note at Ethan's side. It was a weird combination that included an uncontrollable blubbering of emotion, many tears, and a little laughter.

He lifted the pad, stared at it for a moment, and picked up the pen. After a moment, he dropped it at his side.

I picked it up.

Jaz,
I love you, too. When I get this tube out of my mouth, I want a kiss.
I never doubted you.
Ethan

FORTY

JAZ

Day one hundred twenty-one.

I'd never seen a dining table that could seat so many people. I looked around me. The group of people were proof that family may or may not be bound by blood. Some are developed through love, friendship, and a special bond that forms when people close their mouths and open their hearts.

"*You* didn't win shit. I'm tired of it, Mike. Just sick and damned tired. Leave those stories at the door. The girl won the fight. You were just watching," Ripp's dad said.

Ripp dropped his chicken bone onto his plate and glared. "*We* won it."

His dad wagged his fork toward Ripp. "I didn't see you swing a punch. Not one. Jaz won it."

"Is that your name, honey? Jaz?"

I turned toward Ripp's mom, prepared to respond.

"Leave her alone," Ripp snapped. "It's close enough."

Ripp's mom shook her head. "No nicknames at the table."

I shifted my eyes to Ripp. He shrugged. I looked at Dekk. He shrugged. Dekk's wife, Kace, wiped her hands on her napkin and turned toward Ripp's mom.

"It's Beth."

"Yes, Ma'am. It's Beth," I said. "But I don't go by that. I go by Jaz."

She shook her head lightly. "Not at the dinner table, you don't."

I laughed to myself. "Yes, Ma'am."

"See, Mike? You can eat and have manners at the same damned time. Jaz called your mother 'Ma'am'. That's a proper upbringing. I don't know what happened to you. We tried, and tried, but somewhere…"

"Shut it," Ripp said as he reached for the chicken.

"The chicken is great, Mrs. Ripton."

"Thank you Ethan. Eat all you want," she said.

I rubbed my hand along Ethan's thigh. He turned toward me and smiled. His hair was short, but covered all of the scars on his head very well. In another two months it would be as long as it was before they had to shave it, and personally, I couldn't wait.

"So, *Beth*. What's next?" Mike's brother-in-law asked.

"She's going for the other title," Kelsey interrupted.

"Is that right?"

"Yes, Sir. Maybe two more months," I said.

"We'll all have to make it to that one," he said. "Keep us posted."

"I'll let ya know, A-Train," Ripp said.

"No nicknames at the table Michael."

"Alec! Alec! Alec! Alec!" Ripp grunted. "How's that?"

"Mike…" Ripp's wife said. "Play nice."

"They're ganging up on me."

"So, Ethan. We going back to the firing range tomorrow?" Kelsey asked.

Since the incident, Ethan had been enjoying time at the firing range. It seemed to calm his nerves, and it was something easy for him to do and do well.

Some of his progress in recovery was slow, while other things were very rapid. Shooting guns seemed to build his confidence, which was great for keeping his spirits up.

"I'll go the next time, if you don't mind," Alec said.

Ethan pointed the tip of his fork at Alec. "I'd like that. A few pointers from a Marine might get me to beat the old man."

"That jarhead isn't as good as you think. He's lucky," Kelsey said.

"No nicknames at the table," Mikes mom said.

I looked at Kelsey. He sighed heavily. "Jarhead ain't a nickname. It's a derogatory term. I use it with affection. Right, Jarhead?"

Alec rolled his eyes. "Right."

"Beth, when you're done, there's pie."

"Thank you, Ma'am."

"She ain't eatin' no fuckin' pie, Ma. She's in trainin'," Ripp snarled.

"Michael Allen Ripton," his mother snapped back. "That's a bad word. No bad words at the table."

"I'll have a small piece," I said.

"The hell you will," Ripp responded.

His dad poked him with his fork. "Don't argue with her, she'll whip your ass."

"No bad words at the table."

"Ass isn't a bad word."

"It most certainly is."

"It's a body part."

"So's cock," Ripp said. "And we can't use it."

"Michael!"

I grinned.

It was like a circus.

But it was family. And it was the only family I had. After dinner, we sat and talked until long after dark. After all the stories were told, the pie was eaten, and the coffee was gone, I thanked them for my first Sunday dinner.

"Thank you so much for having me," I said.

"I'd say *come anytime*," Mr. Ripton said. "But that's not how we do it. So I'll say this. *See you next Sunday*."

"Okay," I said with a smile. "See you next Sunday."

We bid our farewells and said goodbye to the group.

"You ready, Ethan?"

He nodded. "About to pass out from overeating."

I reached for Ethan's wheelchair. "Thanks again."

As I pushed Ethan toward the door, I thanked God for friends, family, and, as always, for Ethan.

He was the love of my life, and always would be, no matter what. The incident may have broken some couples apart, but it seemed to draw us even closer.

In another month, they were going to be able to operate on his spine and relieve some pressure. We all reserved a little hope that he might be able to feel his legs afterward.

The post-op possibilities, according to the doctor, were only limited by finances. It seemed money could buy the best doctors, the best surgeries, and the best rehabilitation.

Kelsey negotiated 24 million for my next fight. All I had to do was keep winning, and money would be no object.

I loaded the wheelchair into the van, secured it, and gave Ethan a kiss.

Before I closed the van's door, I took a moment to admire him. He was the most handsome man on earth, and he was mine. I couldn't have been any prouder of him. If he spent the rest of his life in the wheelchair, not only would I accept it, I'd embrace it.

But, if money could fix him, I'd spend a mountain of it to do so.

All I had to do was keep winning.

And, if there was one thing I knew how to do, it was win.

EPILOGUE

ETHAN

I parked the truck and glanced to my side. Jaz sat in the passenger seat, blindfolded and mad as hell.

"Can I take it off now?"

"No," I snapped back playfully.

"This is bullshit!" she shouted.

"Just shut it, you mouthy little shit," I said. "It'll be over before you know it."

"I hate surprises."

I got out of the truck, walked to her side of the vehicle, and opened the door. "Just hold on to me." I guided her hand to my shoulder. "There."

I gazed out at the ocean, glad we'd finally reached a point that I was able to take time and drive down to the coast without interfering with her schedule. The last six months had been filled with surgeries, more surgeries, and countless weeks of therapy.

My neck was still going to require some skin grafts for cosmetic reasons, but other than that, I had recovered one hundred percent. I had no intention of returning to boxing immediately, but it was anyone's guess what might happen in the future.

"Why did I have to wear these ridiculous boots?" she asked.

"Because. It's a surprise."

I walked half the distance between where we parked and the edge of the water, stopping about twenty feet from where the ocean met the sand. I reached over, removed her blindfold, and stood back.

The most beautiful woman on earth stood at my side and gazed out at the endless horizon of water.

"You finally made it," I said. "You can take off your boots now. I didn't want you to feel the sand until, well, until I wanted you to."

She stood and stared.

Without speaking, she reached down, removed her boots, and smashed her bare feet into the sand.

She glanced at me and swallowed hard. "It's…"

Her eyes welled with tears. She'd waited a lifetime to make it to the beach, and had sacrificed many potential trips just to make sure I got the surgeries I needed when I needed them the most.

"I know," I said. "It's pretty breathtaking, isn't it?"

"Can I get in it?" she asked.

"You can do whatever you want," I responded. "But before you do, I need to ask you something."

She turned to face me. "What?"

"In the last year, a lot has changed. I feel like we've gained a family at the Ripton's, and I've been working toward fixing things with my father. You've won two championships, and we bought a house. You've got a new Range Rover, and you bought me a new truck. Hell, we don't ever have to do anything to survive. We're set for the rest of our lives."

She smiled a prideful smile.

"But something's missing," I said. "Something big."

"Tell me. Whatever it is, I'll fix it," she said flatly.

"Good. It ought to make this easy, then."

"Just tell me what to do."

I reached into my pocket and removed the ring. "I think it'd be better if I just asked."

She looked at the ring. Before I could muster the courage to continue, a tear rolled down her cheek.

"Beth Briscoe, will you marry me? I can promise you if you do, I'll…"

"Yes," she blurted.

I shook my head and coughed out a laugh. "I wasn't done."

"I was done listening, though. Yes. The answer's *yes*."

"I put together a speech. I was going to--"

"I said yes."

I shook my head and forced out a sigh. "Fine."

I slipped the ring on her finger.

"It's beautiful," she said.

"You're beautiful."

"Thank you." She kissed me. "Can we go down to the ocean now?"

"I thought you'd be more excited."

I am excited," she said.

"About the marriage proposal, not the ocean."

"Shit," she said. "In my mind? I married you a long fucking time ago. Where have you been?"

And she took off running toward the ocean.

I shook my head.

Beth Briscoe.

The craziest woman on earth.

And the love of my life.

www.ingramcontent.com/pod-product-compliance
Lightning Source LLC
Chambersburg PA
CBHW050733180626
46814CB00002B/729